THE
Witchy Worries
OF Abbie Adams

THE
Witchy Worries
OF Abbie Adams

RHONDA
HAYTER

Dial Books for Young Readers

an imprint of Penguin Group (USA) Inc.

DIAL BOOKS FOR YOUNG READERS
A division of Penguin Young Readers Group
Published by The Penguin Group
Penguin Group (USA) Inc., 375 Hudson Street, New York, NY 10014, U.S.A.

Penguin Group (Canada), 90 Eglinton Avenue East, Suite 700, Toronto, Ontario, Canada M4P 2Y3 (a division of Pearson Penguin Canada Inc.) • Penguin Books Ltd, 80 Strand, London WC2R 0RL, England • Penguin Ireland, 25 St. Stephen's Green, Dublin 2, Ireland (a division of Penguin Books Ltd) • Penguin Group (Australia), 250 Camberwell Road, Camberwell, Victoria 3124, Australia (a division of Pearson Australia Group Pty Ltd) • Penguin Books India Pvt Ltd, 11 Community Centre, Panchsheel Park, New Delhi - 110 017, India • Penguin Group (NZ), 67 Apollo Drive, Rosedale, North Shore 0632, New Zealand (a division of Pearson New Zealand Ltd) • Penguin Books (South Africa) (Pty) Ltd, 24 Sturdee Avenue, Rosebank, Johannesburg 2196, South Africa • Penguin Books Ltd, Registered Offices: 80 Strand, London WC2R 0RL, England

The publisher does not have any control over and does not assume any
responsibility for author or third-party websites or their content.

Designed by Nancy R. Leo-Kelly
Text set in Comenius Antiqua
Printed in the U.S.A.
1 3 5 7 9 10 8 6 4 2

Library of Congress Cataloging-in-Publication Data
Hayter, Rhonda.
The witchy worries of Abbie Adams / by Rhonda Hayter.
p. cm.
Summary: Fifth grader Abbie, descended from a long line of witches,
tries to keep her family's magic powers secret from
everyone she knows, until her father brings home a kitten with
some very unusual characteristics.
ISBN 978-0-8037-3468-5 (hardcover)
[1. Witches—Fiction. 2. Magic—Fiction. 3. Friendship—Fiction. 4. Family life—Fiction.]
I. Title.
PZ7.H314942Wi 2010   [Fic]—dc22   2009016743

☙

To my mom,
who saved all my letters
because she always knew
I'd be a writer someday.

☙

∽ Contents ∽

THE Witchy Worries
OF Abbie Adams

CHAPTER 1

My Lucky Sneeze

Come to think of it, the day my brother tried to eat his first-grade teacher turned out to be the same day that my dad brought me home a very, very strange cat.

The truth is, I really shouldn't have gone to school that day. I had a big cold and every time I sneezed, I got a floating attack and had to yank myself down off the ceiling. Once, on a double sneeze, I hit my head on the chandelier really hard. I mean, with a runny nose, a bump on my head, and a propensity (good vocabulary word, huh? Means penchant. Look that up. I had to.) for flying upward really fast, you'd think it would be obvious I belonged home in bed.

But my mom thought my wanting to stay home had something to do with my diorama on the signing of the Declaration of Independence not being quite ready. This was due to the fact that I had gone to ancient Athens to check out the original Olympics rather than sitting around disguised as a pillar while a bunch of old guys in powdered wigs all tried to write their names bigger than each other on some dopey paper. Although I have to admit it was kind of embarrassing how the athletes didn't wear any clothes back then. And the stench of all those big crowds with no real bathrooms made me pretty glad that my parents were living in the twentieth century when I was born. Anyway, the point of all this is that if I *had* been home in bed where I really ought to have been if a person's parents ever listened to her, I wouldn't have stepped outside of my fifth-grade classroom to try to stop a sneeze at the precise moment that my little brother, Munch, ran outside and started morphing into a wolf.

Most people think Munch is short for Munchkin because he's so little and cute, but I actually gave him that name when he was a year and a half old, after having been *bitten* for the fortieth or fiftieth time. His real name is Lazarus, which really only lends itself to the nickname Lazy, so he's probably a lot better off.

Anyway, turns out Munch was a pretty appropriate name because at that moment, he was sprouting hair, growing large teeth, and was about to chomp down on Mr. Merkelson, his first-grade teacher, who was putting him in time-out just outside the front door of his bungalow classroom.

Thinking fast, I clapped three times and yelled out one of those time freeze spells, "STOP, STOP, STOP, CLOCK!!!" on the whole schoolyard, with an extra paralysis hex for Munch. Unfortunately though, that sneeze I had stepped outside to try to squelch came on just then, "AAACHOOO!!!" and I flew up and got caught in the basketball hoop.

Just try getting untangled from a basketball net when you're tall and skinny, your glasses have fallen off your nose, your ponytail is caught up in the hoop, and time has frozen. At least I'm a jeans and T-shirt kind of girl, or else I would have had to deal with my skirt flipping up too.

I had to think way back to my mom's instructions on dosing an object with a humming incantation so I could loosen up the net, while keeping everything else bound up in the time freeze spell. Believe me, just then I wished that I hadn't been worrying about that social studies paper I'd forgotten to write instead of paying closer attention to my mom's lesson. What was it she said anyhow? Hum for two seconds, close one eye, keep a hand on the heart, and blink three times?

Well. No. That wasn't quite right because that just turned the hoop upside down with me in it. It turned out okay though because the sudden rush of pressure to my nose made me sneeze again, causing me to float upward (which in this case was down).

As I dropped down to the schoolyard ground, I avoided a bad bump on the head by landing on my palms and doing the handspring I had just learned to do in gymnastics class. (And my dad thinks that all this human education is a waste for us witches.)

I put my glasses back on my nose and looked over at the frozen scene across the schoolyard. There was Munch in mid-pounce, hanging in the air, poised to take a big chomp out of a horrified Mr. Merkelson.

I had to hurry across the yard because both Munch and Merkelson were starting to quiver a little, a sure sign that my spells weren't holding and, as my mom would probably point out, an even surer sign that I really ought to spend more time on spell technique.

Clapping hard and shouting, "STAY STOPPED, CLOCK!!" I cast the time freeze again, really quickly, and then I snatched Munch out of the scene and brought him out of paralysis with a two-fingered whistle.

Munch's eyes, which were normally very large, very blue, and surrounded with really long lashes, were now small, yellow, and mean-looking. He stood on his hind legs so that he was as tall as I am, turned on me, and growled viciously. Giving him a shake, I called "Munch! Munch!" a few times until I could see his humanity returning. He got smaller and smaller until he was the appropriate size for an undersized first grader, and all the grayish hair covering his body disappeared, except for on his head, where it turned back into Munch's light brown curls. Lastly, those yellow eyes turned blue again and filled up with tears.

"He made me go outside like I was a dog or something," Munch sobbed. "I felt like biting him."

Hey, I understood—I've wanted to chomp down on more than one teacher in my day—but I was the big sister and I had to help Munch get through school without letting anyone know that he was . . . well, a little . . . special.

I gave him a big hug and asked why he was given time-out. "Just wanted her to try yellow!" he wailed.

Well, that didn't make a lot of sense to me, so I had to ask a few more questions, but I finally sorted it out.

Apparently, it had something to do with Munch eating crayons to be funny and trying to force-feed them to Annalise, this little girl he's just crazy about. I calmed him down, told him he'd only have to sit outside for five minutes, and that Annalise probably wasn't mad at him. Then I zapped him up a chocolate cookie, to give him something harmless to chew while he was having his time-out. A quick Hiss-and-a-Whistle forgetting spell on Mr. Merkelson, a *Zap!* back to my own classroom door, then the time freeze reversal . . . and everything was handled nicely.

I watched Mr. Merkelson (he wasn't a bad guy, I had him in first grade myself) gently direct Munch to the bench outside the door, point to his watch to say that he'd be out to get him in five minutes, and then go back inside.

With a little wave to a still sniffling Munch, who was morosely popping chocolate into his formerly fearsome mouth, I went back inside my own classroom. I brandished my handkerchief as I entered, to remind Miss Linegar (rhymes with vinegar) that I had a perfectly valid—actually commendable if you think about it—well, a very good reason to step outside.

CHAPTER 2

My Diorama Dilemma

So anyway, when I got back inside the classroom, Miss Linegar had just closed her day planner and started to stand up. Standing is always kind of a slow business for her because she's been a teacher for about 9,000 years and she's getting on a bit.

She finally got her chair pushed back and her feet under her. "Now boys and girls, it seems we finished our math quickly enough that there'll be time for a few of you to show your dioramas."

I'd been feeling pretty pleased with myself, but when I heard that, my heart hit the floor. Why did everybody have to work so darn fast today? Can't I ever get a break? I know I had a sick look on my face, because I got a sympathetic glance from Callie, at the next desk.

Callie, who's never been late with a project, had a

lovely representation of the Boston Tea Party sitting on top of her desk—and I had exactly nothing sitting on top of mine.

It was nice of Callie to sympathize, but unfortunately, her sympathy didn't make me feel *that* much better because I knew that any moment, my last name starting with an *A* was going to get me called on first like it always does.

Oh, choose a different system sometimes. Try being fair, Miss Linegar.

But sure enough, she called out "Abbie Adams" in that steely, doesn't-expect-much-out-of-me way, and I had to prove her absolutely right by admitting that I didn't have my diorama ready.

Don't think that it didn't cross my mind to cast a little spell or two to get me out of trouble, because it did. But I'm in the fifth grade now and Mom and Dad really don't expect me to make any sort of "mistakes" in that regard. So I had to just stand there, trying to shake off the buzz of magic charge that builds up in my fingers every time I get a little tense, and sheepishly answer Miss Linegar's sarcastic questions.

"Yes, Miss Linegar, I know it was assigned three weeks ago," and, "No, I don't actually *have* any explanation for why it's not ready."

I also had to accept her "consequence" of preparing an extra report on Ben Franklin's participation in the Declaration signing. I didn't mind that too much though. I've gone back to the 1700s and seen Ben Franklin a couple of times, and he's a lot less boring than some of those old guys who signed the Declaration . . . like the second president, John Adams, for instance. What a grump he was. I liked his wife though, and guess what. She had the same name as me.

At least Callie's diorama went over well. Miss Linegar particularly liked the way she used a fishbowl instead of a shoe box, so that the ship carrying the tea was actually floating in water. I was pretty impressed too. Callie's really creative. It's one of the things I like about her, and I also like that she's always my friend even when I have to keep secrets from her.

Sometimes a thing or two might happen that seems a little out of the ordinary. Oh, like the time she happened to come across me in the park near my house, as I was morphing out of being a tree. (It's a witchy thing, you're supposed to learn to be at one with nature . . . by *being* one with nature.) She just caught the tail end of the morph, and I know she was startled and curious, but when she saw that I got flustered at being caught doing something strange, she just threw her arms around me, told me how great it was to run into me this way, and never mentioned a word about it again.

Callie's always thoughtful, unlike my third-grade best friend, Maria. Maria always crossed over to the other side of the schoolyard to avoid me after she happened to see me forget myself for a moment and fly thirty feet through the air to catch Munch as he was falling off his tricycle one day. You see, I forgot all about not doing magic in front of non-witches because it was a really scary moment. Munch was about to fall into the street when a car was driving by.

Oh, and by the way, that was the *only* reason I would have exerted any magical power in front of a non-witch. It was an emergency, okay? And I threw in a forgetting spell on Maria to cover myself. But I was really upset because Munch came so close to getting hurt, so the spell might have gotten a little frayed. Actually, it *must* have gotten frayed, because Maria hasn't spoken to me since. Kind of mean of her, I think; it was my little brother, for heaven's sake. What would *she* have done?

Truth is, it isn't always easy being a witch in a non-witch world, but of course there was that time in

Salem back in the 1600s when that bunch of witches got sort of misunderstood and, well, I don't even want to tell you what happened to them. From that time on, Witch Society went underground and everybody hid the truth about themselves. For instance, there's every possibility that Andrew or Nathaniel in your after-school chess club are witches, but I'll never tell.

After class, Callie came up to me and said, "Hey Abbie, don't feel bad. I'll help you with your diorama, and then you'll be able to get it in tomorrow. Then after that, I think we should change your name to Zorina Zeliker, so you don't have to be first all the time."

Even when I'm feeling really grumpy, which I usually am after an encounter with Miss Linegar, when Callie cracks a joke like that I always feel better. I also knew it would be a lot more fun working on the project with my best friend by studying pictures in books than going back to Philadelphia, circa 1776. One reason is because those powdered wigs they all wore back then really make me sneeze . . . which can get you in trouble if you're supposed to be a pillar. Another thing, people weren't quite as careful about personal cleanliness in those days, and let me tell you something, July in Philadelphia can get hot and humid, and all that sweating in all those heavy clothes they wore back then . . . well, just use your imagination.

I was happy at the idea of bringing Callie home after school. Of course, if I had any idea what was going to happen when we got home, I might have thought differently.

Anyway, my parents are always pleased to see me with Callie. It might be because they think she's a good influence on me. As we headed for the gate, we stopped across the schoolyard to collect Munch. He was playing tag with Annalise, so I guess there were no hard feelings there.

At home, my mom was studying for her real estate license because she's going to go back to work now that Munch has full days at school. I have to admit that when I'm a grown-up, I'm not too sure how fair I'm going to be about not giving myself an unnatural advantage over non-witches in the work force. I mean, sitting and reading all this boring stuff about real estate, when you could just use a little magic and own half the town . . . Oh, I guess I wouldn't ever do anything like that. Actually, I hope that when I grow up I'm just like my mom. Except for the real estate thing; I want to be an actress like my aunt Sophie.

Wait till you meet *her*.

My dad wasn't home yet, so I got some cookies and juice for Callie and me. (Actually, I had to secretly conjure them up. I guess my mom was too busy studying to go shopping.) Then I gave Munch a stern look when he forgot and almost flew up the stairs in front of Callie. Callie and I went up to my room and got to work. We were just making the clock tower of Independence Hall out of a toilet paper roll–Callie's idea–when the whole house went completely dark, a hurricane force wind whipped through the windows, and the front door downstairs slammed open with an enormous crash.

Dad was home.

CHAPTER 3

Dad Has Big News

Clearly, a time freeze spell was called for, to keep Callie locked in a single moment in time, while I went downstairs to see what was happening. I clapped my hands really quickly and yelled, "STOP, STOP, CLOCK!" to slap the spell on Callie, then raced downstairs to alert Dad that we had company.

When I got to the bottom of the stairs, there were still gusts of wind knocking furniture around, pink puffs of smoke were everywhere, and my mom was just walking out of her office door, cracking up at the spectacle my dad was making.

My dad was grinning and zooming around, doing aerial cartwheels with a big bouquet of flowers in his hand that he caused to turn all different colors before he presented them with a big flourish to my mom. He's got brown curly hair like my little brother,

Munch, and it was blowing all over the place. Guess he was happy about something, because when he saw me, he yelled, "Abbie-dabbie-do!" swept me up, and flew me down the hallway and back. Then, *poof,* there was the sweetest little black kitten you ever saw, sitting right in the palm of my hand.

I'd been begging for a cat for months, and I fell in love with this fluffy fuzzball right away ... even though there was something just a bit odd about it. Just *how* odd, you're *not* going to believe, but I'll have to get to that later. Right now, the kitten was staring at my dad and his hijinks, with its little tail puffed out, and furry body shivering all over. I stroked the soft fur until the tremors calmed down.

Just then, Munch, who's six, came sliding down the banister, and my mom had to stomp and yell "SOFT LAND!" really quickly, to conjure up a mattress to catch him at the bottom when he slid right off ... as he always does. Right away, Mom got that look on her face that always means that some consequence is about to follow something Munch or I have done wrong.

"Munch Adams, I have repeatedly told . . ." she started, in her really severe this-is-a-safety-issue tone. That's as far as she got though, because luckily for

Munch, big pink and white puffs of smoke started pumping out of my dad's ears. They were coming out so thickly that my mom's head got practically engulfed in them and she couldn't finish what she'd started to say. Puffs like that were a sure sign that my dad had something exciting he wanted to tell us, so Mom held her tongue . . . for now.

After giving Munch a big hug and a Superman action figure, my dad finally started to calm down so that he could talk to us properly.

I was getting nervous about whether my hastily applied spell upstairs was still holding, but I didn't want to interrupt my dad before I found out what was going on.

"Big news, Adamses! Big news!" my dad kept chortling as he tried to catch his breath. He tends to get a little overexcited sometimes, so my giggling mom finally whispered a little calming spell on him so that he could settle down enough to tell us what was going on. Finally, he sat down on the hall bench, took a breath, and started talking.

"You're going to be very proud of your old dad when you hear this," he said with a huge grin. "*Very* proud."

"I'm always proud of you, Dad." I smiled back. And I am, too, but I wished he'd get to the point because

I was starting to get very worried about Callie. I was thinking that I really ought to have said "STOP" two or three more times, with maybe some louder claps, to seal that spell properly.

Mom urged Dad to spit it out, so finally, after pulling Munch onto his lap and tickling him for a second, Dad settled all the way down. Munch snickered, sneakily blew onto his new toy through his barely parted lips, and then let it go. This was a little spell that sent his action figure hovering high up above my head. He likes to annoy me that way because, of course, I never know when the hovering spell will wear off and the toy will drop right on my head. I didn't care about that right then though, because I was dying to find out what Dad was so excited about.

"Well, you Adamses," Dad began, and then he took a big dramatic pause . . . "I think I just might have discovered the cure for Witch Flu."

Right here is where I should explain a little witchy history. You might have heard the word "mortal" to describe non-witches because humans are mortal, and, well, witches didn't used to be. Mortal, that is. That's right, we used to live forever, or at least for such a long time that nobody knew how old any of us were. (That is, we could live forever as long as we weren't *killed* somehow.) But, back in the 1600s, after the miserable bit of business in Salem, Massachusetts, your average witch got very anxious to blend in.

Apparently, during that period, in which everyone started trying so hard to seem human, the spell for immortality got somehow or other destroyed and erased from history, except for a few stories about it that got passed down. So that's how we ended up with the same life span as everybody else. What's worse, as a result of all this fooling around with life spans and so on, a special new disease that only hits witches developed. It's called Witch Flu. Well, actually it's got some long Latin name, but nobody calls it that. The thing that's really bad about it though is that it can actually rob a witch of his or her magical powers for good. It's been about the worst thing that can happen to a witch for the last three centuries or so, and nobody's been able to find a way to cure it.

Just as my mom opened her mouth to start asking questions, there came a terrific *CLUNK* from upstairs. I knew what it meant. My spell had worn off, and a disoriented Callie had just fallen off the bed.

I gave my dad a quick hug and said, "Gee, that's great, Daddy, but I gotta go for a minute."

I zipped back to my room, helped Callie up, straightened out all her hair braids, whistled a little forgetting spell, and then sat on the bed with her and the toilet paper rolls just as if I'd been sitting with her there all along. There we were, right back where we had been when my dad got home.

I almost got away with it too, except for the fact that from Callie's point of view, a fuzzy little black kitten had just magically appeared in my lap. Ooops. I had forgotten about that. Also, Callie's head was a little sore (due to her fall), and that was confusing her a bit.

She rubbed her head. "Abbie," she said in a creeped-out, wondering sort of tone. "Where did that kitten just *come* from?"

I hated to do it, I really did, but I just pretended that I couldn't imagine what she was talking about and acted like the kitten had been there all the time.

"Oh, didn't I tell you my dad finally told me I could have a cat?" I said, but I sounded all phony and horrible. Even to myself. Maybe even to the kitten, because the little head turned around and the big, round eyes stared right at me.

You hate to deceive your best friend, and I really wouldn't recommend it to anyone, but I just didn't know what else to do.

Luckily, Callie LOVES cats, so she shook off her

headache and her confusion. She picked up and petted the kitten and started murmuring little funny baby phrases like, "Well aren't 'oo just the fuzziest, funniest little furball? Aren't 'oo? Oooh you tweety-pie, you tweety-'ittle pie."

I told her I'd just gotten the kitten and hadn't even named it yet, so we decided to call it Betsy, for Betsy Ross, who sewed the first American flag. Then Callie took a closer look and realized it might be better to pick a different name. So we called him Benjamin, in honor of Ben Franklin.

Funny thing is, I could swear that Benjamin smiled when he got his new name, like he understood what we were saying and approved of the change somehow. Well, it was funny at the time, but it wasn't going to seem so funny later on, I can tell you.

Just then, Munch's Superman action figure, which had been hovering high above me, fell smack down hard . . . right on my head.

CHAPTER 4

Callie Gets Weirded Out

After that stupid toy hit me on the head, suddenly the whole day of trying to control my sneezes, casting spells to help Munch, getting in trouble at school, and hiding who I really was from my best friend just really started to get to me. I couldn't think of how to explain the Superman thing to Callie, and I really didn't want to anyway.

The fuzzy little kitten in my hands started to look all blurry as tears began to burn my eyes. I struggled against an urge to stomp downstairs and kick Munch right in the seat of his pants. I even felt mad at my mom for not having any snacks in the house when I got home and mad at my dad, too, for always making such a big fuss when he gets excited about something.

Across the bed from me, Callie was very quiet, and

it took me a minute to get the nerve to look up and meet her eyes. She didn't look like she was feeling that well. In fact, she was looking a little like Maria did right after the tricycle incident. She didn't seem to know what to say either. Finally, she gave Benjamin another little pat and said, "You know Abbie, I . . . I feel kinda strange right now, and I think maybe I should go home."

Now the tears spilled down my cheeks because I figured I'd lost Callie as a friend, just like I lost Maria. Inside of my head I was yelling, *Oh why? Why did I have to be born a stupid witch in such a stupid witch family anyway?*

Callie got up and stood there for just a second, and then she said, "Abbie, you're my very best friend in the whole world and you know that nothing can ever change that. I just have to go home right now, but we'll sit together at lunch tomorrow."

It was just the right thing to say, and then she even gave me a little hug as she walked out the door.

I sat there sniffling for a bit, and Benjamin stared up at me, like he was trying to figure out what I was feeling. Of course later I would realize . . . well, I'll explain about that soon.

Just then, there was a shuffling noise at the door

behind me, and I turned to see Munch watching me cry. He was all big-eyed and scared-looking.

"I'm sorry, Abbie," he said. "Did the Superman hurt you?"

He looked really sad and worried standing there, and then he made the Superman fly up and hit *him* on the head too, to try to make things even.

Well, I couldn't stay mad at him. I grabbed him and squeezed him really tight and told him it was okay. I even made the Superman fly up again and do a few aerial tricks to make him laugh. And then I sneezed and accidentally hit the ceiling, which made him laugh even harder.

So then I finished up the diorama and wrote a good little report on Benjamin Franklin, which didn't take long. After all, I'd heard him tell enough stories about how he started the first volunteer fire department and first library in Philadelphia and everything that I really didn't need to look anything up. He loved to talk, that Ben Franklin, especially when he was trying to impress the ladies.

Downstairs, Mom, who usually likes to cook in the non-witch way, made an exception and conjured up dinner because she had been so busy with her real estate homework and the PTA fund-raising meeting at our school. My dad was bouncing around, setting the table and talking a mile a minute about the research he'd done in his lab.

"I based it on March Hall's early research at Witchy U," he said to Mom. "I know you don't think much of March Hall, but you can't deny that he's had some innovative ideas, especially in his early work."

My mom was following him around, sorting out the cutlery because he was so excited, he had given everyone either two knives or two forks.

"Yes, but what exactly does the cure consist of?" she asked. Then she looked up and saw me walk in.

Now, my mom can always tell in an instant if something's wrong. It's almost like she's a psychic as well as a witch. Right away she came over to me and asked me if I was okay.

I thought about telling her how much I hated lying to my best friend and how hard I found it fitting in at school and into non-witch life sometimes, but you know, I figured there was really nothing she could do about it. Anyway, I was feeling a lot better since I knew Callie was still my friend, so I just grinned and said I was okay. She gave me one of those deep "Mom looks," as if she was trying to read my mind. Sometimes I think *she* thinks she's psychic too. I guess I must have looked okay though, because she just gave me a little hug.

"All right then, honey," she said. "Would you mind getting the butter out of the fridge?" And we all sat down to dinner.

CHAPTER 5

My Big Fat B

Next day, my cold was a lot better, and I presented my diorama and Ben Franklin report and I've got to say, I felt good about it. Even though I hardly ever seem to manage it, there's something pretty satisfying about having all your work done for once. The kids thought the diorama was really great and they laughed at all the funny things Ben Franklin said, like "A man who is in love with himself will find he has no rivals." Even Ralph Carnaby, who's this kid who gets a big thrill out of embarrassing people, couldn't come up with a snide remark about it.

Anyway, it all went so well that I was as confident as I'd ever been about a project. When I'd finished delivering it, I turned around to smile at Miss Linegar.

She stood up and started shuffling papers, looking

deep in thought. The class was very still, because she always gives grades for projects then and there, right in front of everybody—another of her horrible policies.

"Well, Abbie," she finally said. "I think you did a very nice job and had you turned it in on time, it would certainly have been an A project. As it is though, I'm afraid I can only give it a B."

She still deducted from my marks because the project was late!!! Even though I did the extra report to make up for it!!! I mean, is that fair???!!!

It's really bad of me, I know, but sometimes I can't help wondering how Miss Linegar would enjoy being turned into a toad for five minutes or so. Not that I ever would, of course, but sometimes these little thoughts do creep in.

Later, Callie and I sat together at lunch like she promised and it was almost as if nothing weird had happened between us at all. At first we were a little awkward and I could tell she was waiting to see if there was anything I wanted to explain to her or anything, but when it was clear that there wasn't, she just started yakking as if nothing out of the ordinary had happened.

"Could Miss Linegar have shuffled those papers any

longer before she dropped the B bomb on you?" she said. "Talk about making you sweat. *I* was sweating just watching *you* sweat!"

We ended up having a very nice time together just hanging out through lunch. Callie was all excited because she was signed up for baseball and her first practice was after school the next day. I was happy because I had drama club after school that day.

I happen to love drama club because, as I might have mentioned, my aunt Sophie is an actress and I want to be one too (when I grow up). Later that afternoon, we were doing these exercises where you're supposed to act like an animal. I chose a cat and I tried to move just like Benjamin, scampering up and down the floor by my bookshelves like he did the night before. Of course at that point, I didn't have any idea why he was so interested in my bookshelves. It was just the scampering that caught my eye.

Miss Overton, the director of the drama club, used to be a ballerina about a hundred years ago I think, and she still has perfect posture and is really, really skinny even though she's pretty old now. Anyway, at the end of the session, she stood in the middle of the stage and clapped her hands for quiet. And let me warn you right now, just in case you want to go for a drink of water or something, she can get a little talky.

"Now, my young thespians," she began. "I have consulted with the administrative personnel and it has been ascertained that the schedule for the auditorium will permit a satisfactory rehearsal period for a play, which we can present before the Thanksgiving holiday. I have penned this particular production myself and everyone in the drama club will be able to participate in it, in some form."

Well, she didn't get to say much more for a minute or two because everybody started cheering and yelling about how great it was to be doing a play. My heart started to pound because I really, really hoped that the "form" I got to participate in was not building sets or running the lights. I wanted to be IN the play. Really badly.

Miss Overton went on, "Now, I do hope that as the author, I'm not being too self-congratulatory if I remark that there are many rather clever speaking parts and a rich assortment of colorful character turns. Consequently, everyone's talents will be *amply* and, if I do say so myself, *ably* represented."

Okay, let me just tell you now, so that you don't die of suspense like I nearly did. Here's the big news. From all the classes we'd done, she had already figured out who should play what part. And guess who got the biggest one. Me.

Are you ready for this? The play was going to be about a girl who doesn't believe in magic. Well, if you happened to ever get the word "irony" wrong on any of your vocabulary tests, there's a good example of it. I couldn't wait to get home to tell my mom that the last person in the whole school who would disbelieve in magic was cast to play a girl who *didn't* believe in it. I was also really hoping we could call my aunt Sophie to tell her, too.

CHAPTER 6

Meet Aunt Sophie

When Munch and I got home, I ran right to my mom to tell her about the play. She laughed really hard when she found out about the part I got, and when I asked if we could tell Aunt Sophie about it, she got right on the phone and passed it to me.

I told Aunt Sophie the big news about the play and then I told her about how my character didn't believe in magic . . . and as soon as I did, there was a terrific *WHOOOSSHH* of air and I felt as if cold fingers were playing up and down my spine. All of a sudden, it looked as if silvery snow was falling in the living room for just a second and there was a sound like tinkling bells. Aunt Sophie was popping in.

My aunt Sophie is a really well-known actress and right now, she was starring in a TV movie about the American Civil War, so she was wearing one of those long, wide dresses with a hoop underneath the skirt. As she materialized, her hoop skirt knocked my mom's favorite vase off the coffee table, but Aunt Sophie just gave it a little zap from her left pinkie and it flew right back onto the table safely before it even hit the floor.

"Oh Abbie, my lovey-doo! What a scream!" she laughed, and she swept me up in her arms and gave me a big kiss, giving another little zap with her pinkie to get the lipstick off my cheek afterward. As she spun me around, her long, silky blond hair whipped around behind her, like in a shampoo commercial.

"You make sure to tell me exactly what the date of the performance is," she went on. "Because I wouldn't miss it for the world, not for the *world!!*"

Then she zapped a little tickling spell on Munch and flew over to my mom. "Matty!!" (She tends to speak in exclamation marks like that.) "Matty!! That new stylist just showed me the cutest cut that would look absolutely adorable on you and you cannot possibly live without it another minute!"

And then she zapped this flippy sort of hairstyle onto my mom's shoulder-length brown hair. Blowing kisses all around as a ringing cell phone materialized in her hand, she laughed as she looked at the number and said, "Oh, good . . . about time. Gotta take this. Love you! Love you! Love you!" Then she disappeared in another silvery blizzard.

So that's my aunt Sophie. Usually she stays longer, but she was in the middle of a movie shoot and didn't have a lot of time. That's one of the really good parts about being a witch though. You don't have to wait for airplanes and things when you feel like seeing someone. And I always feel like seeing my aunt Sophie.

My mom was just checking out her new hairstyle in the mirror over the fireplace and trying to decide if she liked it, when Munch started a little ballgame with his plastic baseball players. Some of Munch's skills are not too well developed yet, so his toy pitcher made a really bad throw and the marble Munch had given him as a ball clipped me hard, right on my ankle bone. I was watching my mom, so it took me by surprise and I kind of cried out.

"AAAhh!"

Munch's eyes got really big and he said, "Oh no, Abbie. Are you going to cry again?"

At that, my mom turned around to me and asked, "When were you crying, sweetheart? What happened?"

Somehow, it all seemed so complicated to try to

explain, and my mom was worried enough about her real estate test and about not being at home as much as before. Anyway, though part of me wanted to talk to her about how hard it was to keep all these darn secrets all the time, another part of me wanted to forget about that stuff for now and just be happy about my play.

So I didn't really lie. I would *never* lie to my mom, but I didn't exactly tell the whole truth either. I just said something like, "Oh, Munch's Superman bonked me kind of hard on the head last night" . . . which was true, you have to admit.

"Oh, Munch," said my mother. "I've spoken to you about tormenting your sister with those hovering spells, haven't I?"

Now I felt bad because it looked like I might be getting Munch in trouble. I hurried to say, "It's okay, Mom. We worked it out between us."

My mom loves it when we do what she calls "resolving conflicts appropriately," so she just smiled, looked back and forth between us approvingly, and said, "That's good, then."

Then she completely changed the subject. "Abbie, when you get the script for your play I'd love to help you learn your lines."

That night, Mom cooked dinner in the non-witch way. I really like when she does this, because when I get home from school, the whole house is full of good smells that make me so happy to be home for dinner. The food's just as good when she does it the witchy way, but you just can't beat those smells when you first get home. Tonight it was roast chicken with mashed potatoes and gravy. Yum.

At dinner, my dad seemed sort of worried, like he was thinking about other things. He didn't even notice my mom's flippy hairstyle.

My mom stood right in front of him and said, "Um. Helloooo?" in that sing-songy way she has that lets you know something's expected of you.

I mean, it *was* a completely different style from how she usually wears it, and Dad really ought to have noticed.

Dad finally looked up and smiled.

"Oh, that's pretty, Tildy," he said.

Even though he complimented her, I could tell he probably thought it looked more like Aunt Sophie's style than my mom's. My mom could tell too . . . I think she'd been kind of feeling that way about it as well. She didn't zap it right away, but as dinner continued, she just let it slowly unflip and rearrange itself back to her straight shoulder-length style, which is a lot more natural-looking. I was sort of relieved actually because I like the way my mom wears her hair. Anyway, I think that kind of fancy hairstyle looks better on people who are all dressed up, which my mom hardly ever is.

So, we kept eating dinner and Dad didn't say a thing and just kept getting lost in his thoughts again. It wasn't until Munch grew an extra pair of hands so he could grab two more cookies for dessert that Dad finally looked up and laughed . . . even though he made Munch put the cookies back.

"Good try, buddy," he said as he passed the cookie plate to Munch, so Munch could replace the cookies.

I went to bed early and snuggled up with Benjamin and a book. He was very cute, lying there with me, cocking his head as if he was trying to make sense of the words on the page himself. I was reading this great Sherlock Holmes story, but I fell asleep before I got to the last page, where Sherlock always makes all his deductions and solves the crime. Strangely though, when I woke up in the morning, the book *was* open to the last page and Benjamin was lying on it sound asleep. I was starting to get a peculiar feeling about that kitten.

CHAPTER 7

An Unexpected Visitor

A few days later, when Munch and I got home from school, I found a note from my mom saying she had to run out for a few minutes and to help myself and Munch to some peanut butter crackers and milk. I don't really like peanut butter crackers all that much, but my mom is stubborn about us eating too much sugar, so that was the snack for today.

"Let's conjure up some honey to drizzle on them," Munch suggested.

"Aw, if Mom wanted us to have honey she would have drizzled it on them herself," I answered dutifully, even though I was really wishing she had.

Munch's chin started to stick out a little bit in his mad face, but all of a sudden Benjamin came scampering up to us, bumping his head into our shins to say hello, and we both got distracted by him.

Benjamin went racing up the stairs and Munch and I couldn't help but laugh at how fast his little legs could go. We ran up and chased after him, but when we got to my room, there was a surprise.

Every book that had been sitting on my bedside table was now lying on the floor and was open as if someone had been reading it. Not only that, Benjamin was jumping up and down in front of my bookshelves as if he was trying to pull down more books. He's just a tiny little kitten, so he wasn't getting very far.

I looked at Munch, who sounded unimpressed. "Benjamin wants to read," he said.

Then Munch walked across the hall to his own room pretty quickly, as if he was afraid that he'd have to stick around to read too. Munch likes being read to, especially by my dad, who always makes the illustrations come to life, but he hates reading himself.

Well, of course I didn't really think that Benjamin wanted to read, but I pulled down the book he seemed to be jumping up for, which happened to be an illustrated volume about science fair projects.

As soon as I took the book down, Benjamin started to purr, and when I opened it up on the bed for him, he gave me a little lick of thanks. Right away, he sat his little self down and started moving his head back and forth as if he really was reading the book. In way less time than I would have taken to finish the page, he jumped up and turned the page by pushing it across with his little padded front paws. Then he sat down to start all over. It was kind of adorable really, and I figured he was just copying what he'd seen me do, when . . .

BOOM!!!

There was a big clap of thunder and my bed suddenly lifted up and slammed back down, tossing Benjamin right onto the floor.

"Oh my," said someone who had just materialized under my bed.

Knowing what you know about my family now, you might not think it's so unusual to have people come out of nowhere right in the middle of your bedroom. Actually though, it's not considered very good manners to arrive unannounced in somebody's house unless you're close family.

To tell you the truth, I felt pretty nervous about poking my head under the bed to see who was there— especially since there was a little groaning and moaning going on. I wished Mom or Dad were home, and

I considered getting Munch and running out of the house with him. I mean, you may not know this, but not everybody in the Witchy World is quite as nice as you might want them to be. And when someone's not nice *and* has magic powers, well . . . it can be pretty scary. Munch and I are also not supposed to talk to adults we don't know unless we have a parent with us–just like I'm sure you're not supposed to either.

Something was happening to the air, too. It was shimmering and the temperature kept shifting between hot and cold. Something weird definitely was going on and I turned to intercept Munch, who was just running in as Benjamin was racing out.

"Hey, Abbie, I cast a hair spell just like Aunt Sophie's!!!" he yelled excitedly, pointing to his large pink Mohawk. Then he noticed something was wrong too.

I'd just decided the best thing to do was to take Munch outside until Mom could get home, when the bed rose up with a couple of weak little jumps and an elderly man rolled out from under it. He seemed dazed and very upset and I realized that he was one of my dad's patients. I had recently met him in Dad's waiting room.

"Oh my. Oh my. I, I don't know what happened," he stammered. "I was on my way to, oh where was I going? Oh, well, it will come to me. Did I take a dizzy turn?" Then he looked sort of scared and like he might cry or something.

It was pretty clear that he was harmless, so I helped him sit on my bed, got him a drink of water, and rushed to the phone to call my dad's office. Dad zapped himself right home and when he emerged out of the blue sparkles he travels in, the old man looked really relieved to see him. "Oh my, Dr. Adams," he said, his voice trembling. "I . . . I . . . I just don't know what happened."

Listen. If you ever get sick, my dad is definitely the one you want to call, because in about two seconds flat, he had the frightened old man feeling a lot better.

"Mr. Heatherhayes," Dad said. "I know it's worrying, but this sort of unexpected locale jump is a side effect we're just starting to see with the new serum. I promise you there's absolutely nothing to worry about. Now, I'm going to summon your son and he'll take you right home. You have a cup of tea and lie down and you'll feel much better before you know it."

Dad's voice was so reassuring that Mr. Heatherhayes calmed right down. In just a moment, his son, who's a guy about my dad's age, popped in and took over his father's care. After talking with my dad briefly, he zapped himself and Mr. Heatherhayes home.

Dad took a moment to ruffle my hair and say, "Abbie Dabbie, you did exactly the right thing. That must have been kind of scary, but I'm proud of how you handled yourself."

He also complimented Munch on his big pink Mohawk . . . though he did tell him it was time to change it back.

Munch, who, as you might have guessed by now, sometimes doesn't listen quite as well as he should, brought back his brown curls right away. He could see that my dad was looking really serious.

It's a funny thing about my dad. There are times when he gets so silly and fun that he seems just like another kid. But when he's taking care of patients, or thinking about his work, or anything else really serious, he's a different guy entirely. It's okay though because I like him both ways.

When old Mr. Heatherhayes and his worried-looking son were gone, my dad did a clearing spell on the air. Then he swooped his hands around to create an anti-infection wave over Munch and me and finally got everything back to normal.

When he had finished, Dad sank down on my bed, looking deep in thought. You can always tell when my dad has a lot on his mind because black smoke starts chugging slowly out of his ears. Benjamin came back in and rubbed up against his legs and he didn't even notice.

Pretty soon, it felt as though Dad had forgotten we were there in the room with him, so I picked up Benjamin and took him and Munch back to Munch's room. I was worried about my dad, but I did happen to note that Benjamin seemed to look back longingly at my science book, which had fallen off the bed onto the floor. I'm telling you . . . peculiar. I would have mentioned it to my dad, but he seemed to have a lot on his mind just then.

Things looked pretty funny in Munch's room because all his action figures had ridiculous hairstyles. For instance, his Superman now had multicolored spikes. I guess Munch had been practicing on his toys before he cast the pink Mohawk spell on his own hair.

Benjamin jumped up onto Munch's bookshelf and I wasn't completely sure, but it looked as if he got a disdainful look on his fuzzy little face when he saw that it was full of picture books and beginning readers.

When I walked back across the hall to peek in on my dad, he was sitting on my bed with another man. They were both so focused on their conversation that they didn't even notice me.

The other man was really tall and skinny with lots of fluffy white hair and he was wearing a suit and had a briefcase at his feet. He was so stiff and formal and businesslike that he actually looked kind of silly sitting squeezed in beside my dad on my frilly pink bed under my Hermione Granger poster.

There was nothing silly about the man's tone though or the way my dad was intently listening to everything he said. I was certainly curious, but I didn't want to make a pest of myself, so all I managed to overhear was something my dad said about the "serum provoking involuntary responses" before I went back into Munch's room.

When I got there, I could hear Mom arriving home. Munch and I raced each other down the stairs, to try to be the first one to tell her what had happened. He ended up getting there first because I'm just too good a big sister to run him over.

"I'm telling it! I'm telling it!!" yelled Munch as he slid along the front hall in his sock feet.

When Mom had finally sorted out our two stories, she got this really concerned look on her face and went up to see my dad and that man. They stayed in my room a long time, talking in low voices. When they came out, they all looked worried. Not so worried though that Mom forgot to remind me it was time to do my home-work . . . with a strong suggestion that I take extra time after my schoolwork to focus on the spell technique exercises she'd been assigning me recently.

I went into my room and sat at my desk to work on my math problems, but I had a hard time concen-trating. I mean, it had just been a few days since my dad was so excited about his discovery of a cure for Witch Flu. But here, apparently, was a case of some-thing going wrong with it right in our own house, and my dad certainly hadn't been turning any aerial cartwheels lately.

Before I knew it, a whole hour had gone by, Mom was telling us that dinner was ready, and I still hadn't finished the first page of math problems. And I still had three more pages to go. Miss Linegar isn't one of those teachers who believes in leaving kids a whole lot of free time.

That little magic charge started to build up in my fingers again and I have to admit, the temptation to finish the work magically was really strong but I managed to overcome it. I'd just have to finish the math after dinner, and leave Mom's spell technique homework for the weekend.

CHAPTER 8

I Have a Little Problem with Bees

The next Tuesday was the first rehearsal for the play and as soon as we got to the auditorium, Miss Overton handed out our scripts.

"And here, for Abbie, is the role of our little skeptic," she said. "There'll be quite a commitment required in order to memorize all your lines, dear, but I know we can count on you."

When I looked at the script, I couldn't believe how many lines I had and I got so excited that I had to keep shaking my fingers to get rid of that pesky magic charge. Miss Overton happened to notice me, but luckily she just thought I was doing a relaxation exercise.

"Hear hear, young thespians!" she called out. "Please observe how Miss Adams has admirably absorbed her lessons here and is practicing the relaxation techniques so necessary to the dramatic craft. It would behoove you all to follow her praiseworthy example. Let us start as she has, by shaking out the tension from our hands."

Miss Overton tends to use words like "behoove" and "praiseworthy" when she could just say something like they *ought* to follow my *good* example. In fact, I've never heard her use a ten-cent word when a five-dollar one would do.

Anyway, she got the whole cast shaking out their hands and feet and rolling their necks around and breathing in "big sighs" and stuff in order to relax. I ought to have felt a little ashamed of taking credit for something I wasn't really doing and pretending to be worthy of praise and everything. But heck, I get in trouble enough for stuff I'm *not* responsible for, so I figured I'd take a free compliment for a change.

I gotta tell you, the play was fantastic, and even though I got the most lines, other people's parts looked like a lot of fun too. Everybody else was going to play a lot of different characters and even the furniture and things.

This guy Caetano, who's also in my gymnastics

class, was going to get to play Peter Pan. He'd fly in
on ropes through a window for one scene. Calvin
and Dennis, who are in Miss Linegar's class with me,
were doing a little excerpt from *Alice in Wonderland*.
Calvin played the mushroom that the caterpillar sits
on, while Dennis played the caterpillar. And it was
really funny because in our version, the mushroom
complains the whole time about how much the
caterpillar weighs. He also keeps interrupting the conversation with these huge, hacking coughs because
of the smoke from the caterpillar's pipe.

See, the plot of the play was that this girl who
doesn't believe in magic (that would be *moi*, your
humble narrator) falls asleep while reading a book.
She dreams that she wanders into a magical kingdom
where characters and scenes from books come alive.
In the end, she comes to realize that books are full of
magic that anyone can use.

Of course it's true about books having magic, and
I really like books a lot, but just between you and me,
there's magic and then there's *magic*, if you know
what I mean.

Anyway, it was a really good play with lots of funny
parts, and as Miss Overton put it, some "eerie and
fantastical sections" that were going to have special

sound and lighting effects and dry-ice smoke and everything. I *love* that stuff!!!

You know, before Miss Overton used it, I didn't know that "fantastical" was even a word, but apparently it is. Inside, I was thinking that I could certainly show everybody a touch of "eerie and fantastical" but naturally, being very mature for my age, I restrained myself.

The first time I got up and started acting though, I got this really strange sensation that I didn't know what to do with my hands. I mean, if you're just hanging around talking to your friends, your hands aren't something you even think about, are they? But something about getting up on a stage with everyone watching you suddenly makes you feel as if your hands are two big clubs hanging around by your sides. You get this weird feeling that you really ought to *put* them somewhere.

The other strange thing about having a lot of people watching you is that *you* feel like you're watching yourself too . . . and sometimes what you see doesn't look too good. Well, today it was just Miss Overton watching, but I knew there were going to be a lot more people later.

In the scenes where I didn't have any lines and I

didn't have to hold my script, I started to shift from one leg to another and stick my hands in my jeans pockets and on my hips and up in my ponytail and behind my back until Miss Overton finally said something.

"I beg your pardon, Miss Adams. But what in heaven's name are you trying to accomplish with all that fidgeting?"

Well then, after she said that, I got so tense and awkward that a little tiny burst of magic charge built up and actually shot right out of my fingers before I got a chance to shake it off. It zapped a barefoot Michael Reid, who was playing an apple tree, right on the big toe.

I instinctively said, "Excuse me," like a polite witch should, but luckily no one heard me because of all the noise Michael was making. He thought he'd been stung by a bee and got all upset, jumping up and down and shaking his foot all over the place and causing a big fuss.

Soon all the kids in the club (except yours truly) were screaming and running around yelling, "Bees! Bees!!"

When I gave it a second thought, I jumped around and started yelling about bees too, just to cover myself.

"Beeees!!!"

Miss Overton gave a big sigh and said, "Well, this looks like an opportune moment to draw rehearsal to a close."

I couldn't have agreed more.

CHAPTER 9

Do Witches Face Instinction?

Back at home, I was just considering putting in an urgent call to Aunt Sophie for acting advice, when Dad called Munch and me into the living room. He was holding Mom's hand as he said, "Kids, I'm very sorry to have to tell you this, but the cure I thought I'd found for Witch Flu is having some serious side effects on a few of my patients. I'm afraid we'll all have to prepare for more unexpected visitors like Mr. Heatherhayes."

It seems the serum Dad had been giving people was bringing back their lost magical powers all right but not completely, just sort of every now and then. Anyway, Dad said he's still hoping that the effect will eventually smooth out and that he was conferring with an expert in the field, who I guessed was that man with the white hair I saw with Dad in my room.

The really weird thing about the serum Dad had given his flu patients was that it seemed to be making people involuntarily zap back to the source of the medicine (my dad) every time. Apparently Dad's office is jammed with witches who suddenly materialize out of nowhere, seeming kind of confused. People who are *really* sick just sort of zap around to places where Dad has been or *might* be, which is how Mr. Heatherhayes ended up at our house.

Gee, I can't imagine what it would be like to have your powers controlling you, instead of you controlling your powers—although I guess that little incident with the "bee sting" in drama club does kind of give me a clue.

"Daddy, if you don't find a cure for it, will witches become instinct?" asked Munch worriedly as he climbed up into my dad's lap.

"That's *extinct*, buddy." My dad smiled, kind of sadly. "It's not going to be as bad as all that, and hey, since there's a doctor in the house, you and Abbie will get an anti-infection wave every night."

Dad swooped his arms up to bathe us in the wave and then we followed Mom into the kitchen to help with dinner. The refrigerator door popped open. Phil and Felix, the Schnitzler boys, fell out, looking very startled. They each had an end of a little toy car, as if they'd been in the middle of fighting over it.

"Hi, guys," said Munch, and gave them a little wave because he knew Phil from Witch Preschool.

Mom explained what was happening to the confused brothers, cleaned up the leftover pumpkin pie that had gotten on them in the fridge, and zapped them both back home.

And it was the last piece of pie too, darn it.

CHAPTER 10

We Find Out Something about My Kitten

After school the next day, Callie came home with me and Munch again, and we played catch in the backyard for a bit while Munch did his homework with Mom.

I was doing pretty good at catching for a while, but then I missed a hard pitch Callie threw to me and it nearly hit Benjamin, who had hauled my science homework sheets out of my backpack and was spreading them out on the patio by sliding on them like they were little kitty sleds. I yelled at him to watch out, but he didn't even look up as the ball nearly hit him.

Okay. Now there was no doubt about it, that cat was actually sorting those papers and something was *definitely* peculiar about him. Luckily, there was a bush blocking Callie's view and she couldn't see Benjamin, so I didn't have to make myself feel miserable by having to hex her *again.*

I was really curious about Benjamin now. After Mom sent Callie home so I could study for my spelling test, I picked him up and took a deep look into his eyes. And what I saw was so shocking it was as if I'd stepped off a pier into icy water.

Benjamin wasn't really a kitten at all. He was a *boy!*

I cupped him in my hands and ran into the house to ask Mom to take a look at him. She picked him up, looked into his eyes, and gasped. "Oh my!" she said. "Oh my!"

Mom pulled on her ring finger and whistled to summon my dad, and he zapped right home. He took a hard look at Benjamin too. Then he got so upset to think that he hadn't noticed an enchanted person in his own house that he had to fly around the room a few dozen times, chugging black smoke, just to cool off.

"Marley, where did you say you got Benjamin?" asked Mom as she settled Benjamin onto her best chair.

"Well, well, you know, Tildy, my office back door was open and he just, he just wandered in," huffed my dad nervously, waving away the smoke. "I asked around all over the building but no one knew whose he was, so I figured he was just a stray who would need a good home. I never dreamed . . . I never dreamed he wasn't a real cat. Can you believe it?"

My parents looked more upset than I'd ever seen them. Even my mom, who's usually really cool in upsetting situations, kept having to flick magic charge out of her fingers. She just kept saying over and over again, "Oh his poor mother. She must be worried sick."

Dark smoke was pouring out of my dad's ears so fast and thick that it was getting hard to see, and my mom had to keep muttering breezy spells to clear out the fog.

Munch and I had never seen our parents like this, and Munch was starting to look scared. I took him into his room and told him not to worry.

"You know what, Munchie?" I said. "It's just a medical issue and hey, if anybody can cure Benjamin, it's Dad."

Once Munch seemed a little better, we both snuck back into the living room, where it looked like Benjamin was getting excited about all the activity. As soon as he saw me, he scampered across the room and jumped up into my arms.

I cuddled him and whispered to him. "It's okay," I said. "It's all going to be okay."

I looked deep into my little kitten's eyes again. It's hard to explain because it's not as if I really *saw* anything inside the slits of Benjamin's yellow cat eyes, but I got sort of an impression, if you know what I mean. (And if you're not a witch, you probably don't.) It was a hazy image of a boy of around thirteen, a big-headed sort of kid, with bright blue green eyes, who didn't seem able to stand still. The funny thing is, he didn't look scared or worried, as I most certainly would have been if I woke up one day to find out that I was a cat. No, he looked sort of . . . well, *intrigued,* as if all of this was incredibly interesting to him.

I know it sounds weird to describe what he was wearing, since I didn't actually *see* the kid, but somehow I knew that he wasn't in modern clothes. He looked like he was wearing something you might have seen in a picture of somebody back in those days when they used to make kids wear way too much. I've done a little time traveling back to the 1800s, which is when it looks like this kid might have come from, and I came away from the experience feeling really sorry for kids back then. The girls' clothes were just ridiculous, I don't even want to talk about them, they had to wear so much. But even the boys had to sweat all day in high collars and ties and stiff, tight jackets and hats or caps in all weather. They must have found it impossible to run around or do anything fun like chase a ball. And don't even get me started about how dumb those big swimsuits were back then. It's a wonder everybody didn't drown.

While Mom and Dad were running around consulting books and arguing about spells with each other, Munch took a turn to look into Benjamin's eyes. After just a moment, he smiled in at him and said, "Oh. Hi, Tom," really loudly, as if he were yelling down into a deep well or something.

As soon as Munch said it, I knew somehow that he was right, that the boy's name wasn't Benjamin at all, but Tom.

You know, Munch is a funny kid. Just when you think he's still a baby and you can't expect much out of him, he surprises you by understanding something better than you do yourself.

After he heard his real name, Tom bumped his

head up against both of us and purred as loudly as I'd ever heard him purr. I think I know how he felt. Have you ever tried to explain something you're feeling to somebody and then you finally realized they understood exactly what you meant, and were maybe even feeling the same way themselves? That was how I figured Tom was feeling just then. It's the way Callie and I feel about things with each other all the time. My mom's good that way too.

Dad had all kinds of witchy medical books out and Mom was calling around to friends of hers to see who might have been visiting the nineteenth century lately. And by the way, isn't it annoying how the 1800s is called the *nineteenth* century instead of the *eighteenth* century? Sometimes it feels as if things are arranged just so Miss Linegar will have things to correct me on.

That tall, skinny man showed up again, popping right into the living room with his briefcase already open.

"Oh. Thank you for coming, Dr. March Hall," said Mom.

It's funny, just for a moment, I thought she said Dr. March *Hare* like that crazy hare at the tea table in *Alice in Wonderland.*

While the grown-ups were busy in another room, Munch turned himself into a mouse so Tom could chase him, but Tom didn't seem interested. He had jumped up on the sideboard to push his little paw against the light switch. Off and on. Off and on. He'd crane his sweet little furry head around every time he did it so he could watch the lights in the chandelier go on. I laughed because it was so cute, but then I bit my lip because now that I realized he was a kid and not a cat, I figured I'd better be careful not to look like I was making fun of him.

Dr. March Hall and Mom and Dad didn't seem to be getting too far in figuring out how to change Tom back and get him home to his parents, and after Mom zapped Munch and me a pizza, they went right back to work on it. Dr. March Hall seemed to be the one doing most of the talking, and he had this really loud, kind of overpowering voice.

"As Andropov/Yeshinsky report, in the addendum to their third study on antagonistic transmogrification . . ."

Honestly, it got a little hard to listen to it after a while because he just kept talking and talking and it seemed like no one else could get a word in edgewise.

Munch and I were eating the pizza in the living

room while the adults worked in Mom's office. I thought it might be nice to hear a little music to drown out Dr. March Hall, so I turned on the CD player, which, as it happened, had one of Munch's heavy metal CDs in it.

Well, I nearly fell off of my chair at Tom's reaction.

All the fur on his back stood on end, his tail puffed out to three times its size, and he leaped a foot up in the air, yowling as though I'd set his feet on fire. I figured the music was a bit too much for him. I mean, heavy metal certainly isn't to everyone's taste, it certainly isn't mine. So I turned the CD right off.

With his eyes looking enormous and round, Tom quieted his trembling and seemed to gather his nerve to approach the CD player. He sniffed it and patted the buttons with his little paws and looked at me as if he wanted me to do something. So I turned the volume down much lower and pressed play again. This time Tom shook his head and started staring at every inch of the player in turn, as if he was trying to figure out how it worked. Very quickly he figured out where the volume button was, and he kept turning it up really loud, until it hurt Munch's and my ears and I'd turn it back down again.

After I finished my homework, Tom was still examining the CD player and trying all its buttons. It was late, so I turned off the music, picked him up, laid him out on my bed with a good book, and went to sleep. In the morning when I woke up, he'd already gone off somewhere.

CHAPTER 11

Munch's Meltdown

Munch woke up grumpy. He was mad because my mom got him up a little late and told him he'd have to hurry, and Munch HATES to hurry.

He took as long as he possibly could to get out of bed, until my mom (after asking him nicely about a hundred times) finally raised her voice at him and then he got mad at her for yelling. Unfortunately, as you may or may not have noticed by now, Munch doesn't always manage his anger too well.

First thing he did after Mom yelled was turn himself into a teddy bear and hide among his stuffed animal collection at the foot of his bed. Next, after my mom zapped that spell away and pulled him onto his feet, he turned himself into a bird and she had to slam down the window so he didn't fly out of it.

"Munch, honey, please," she said, much more

nicely than I would have under the circumstances.

I hate when Munch gets like that. Especially in the mornings. When he melts down before school, he makes it so we have even less time to have breakfast and get ready. In fact, I don't mind admitting, there are times I wish I was an only child. By now he was really starting to get on my nerves, so I yelled at him.

"Munch, you monster! Just get dressed already why don't you!"

Then he had the nerve to bonk me on the head with his Superman again. Can you believe it? After he was so sorry for doing it the other night? It's a good thing I'm so much more mature than he is, that's all I can say, because all-out war could have erupted.

Finally, even my mom lost it.

"Munch Adams! If you don't stop morphing this instant you will not be going to see Jimi Hendrix at Woodstock!"

Woodstock was some big outdoor rock concert way back in 1969 and Jimi Hendrix was a guitar player who's still on half of Munch's T-shirts even today, so I guess he was pretty good. Anyway, Munch, who's learning to play guitar himself, certainly didn't want to miss him, so he *finally* brushed his teeth and got dressed.

By then we were late for school and I had to hurry out the door with him as we both stuffed down bananas and granola bars instead of the oatmeal Mom had been planning to cook for us. I know my mom loves us, so I don't take stuff like this personally, but I did happen to notice she looked distinctly relieved to get us out of the house.

My friend, there's nothing worse than arriving late at Miss Linegar's class. You know what she does, just to make it a completely horrible experience? She *locks* the door so you can't just open it quietly and slip in. No, you've got to knock and then she has to assign somebody the "privilege" of opening the door, to see who it is, and of course everyone in the whole class turns around to stare at you.

Once you're inside, you have to go up to Miss Linegar's desk to apologize for your tardiness. Then, if she really wants to give you a hard time (and she always does), she'll ask for an explanation as to why you're late. Which is what she did on this particular morning.

"Abbie, the bell rang five minutes ago. How is it that you're just arriving?"

And what could I say? That my little brother went on a morphing rampage and it put me behind schedule? That'd go over big. So I mumbled something about having slept late and she sighed and told me to hurry up and sit down.

"Now, boys and girls, let's all forget the interruption and get back to clearing your desks for the spelling test."

Spelling test?? Oh no! I knew I'd forgotten something the night before, in all the excitement about Tom. It was really hard words that week too, like "fasinate," or "facinate," or however the heck you spell it.

Well, you can guess how I did on the test. And I had really meant to study for it too. Oh, by the way, in case you ever need to know, "fascinate" is spelled with both an s *and* a *c*. Wish somebody had told me. And can I ask you, what is with this silent letter thing anyway? What is the point of it exactly? See what I mean about it seeming like things are designed just to give Miss Linegar ammunition against me?

At recess with Callie, I really felt like telling her all about Tom but I knew I couldn't, even though it was driving me crazy. I considered telling her about it and then putting a forgetting spell on her, but you're not supposed to hex people unless it's absolutely necessary. Besides, I already felt bad about how many times I'd had to hex her for other things.

Instead, I just complained to Callie about Munch and what a monster he was sometimes. She looked across the yard at how *adorable* he looked, playing tetherball with Annalise, laughing whenever the ball bonked his cute curly little head, and I could tell she really didn't get it. Callie is an only child, as I think you might be able to guess.

At least I got to go to drama club after school again, but Miss Overton was a bit disappointed in me because I hadn't learned any of my lines yet. I felt bad about it too, but the truth is I felt better having to hold the script so my hands weren't flopping around like they had been the other day.

We worked really hard at the rehearsal and I got a lot of my lines memorized as we went along, but today things broke down when Calvin and Dennis starting goofing around during the mushroom scene.

"Concentration, children! Concentration!" Miss Overton yelled as the drama group started to get a little out of control.

When Calvin, the mushroom, collapsed completely under Dennis's weight, everybody got the giggles so bad that she ended rehearsal a few minutes early.

Maybe we didn't get as much work done as we should have. Still, it was an awful lot of fun.

CHAPTER 12

Mom and Dad Get Serious

On the way home, Munch was just as cheerful and happy as if he'd been a total angel all day long. I held a grudge for a little while, due to the Miss Linegar torture, but it's hard to stay mad at Munch too long, so I finally forgot about it.

I hurried him along and he let himself get hurried this time, which I was glad about, because I really wanted to get home to see what was happening with Tom.

When we walked in the front door, we almost tripped over the Schnitzler boys, who suddenly materialized right in front us, with homework papers flying around them. They were grappling over something Felix had in his hand.

"I need the red crayon!"

"I had it first!"

The Schnitzlers looked kind of surprised when

they realized they were back at our house. I happened to know where they lived because I'd been with Mom when she dropped off Munch at a birthday party there last year, so I just gathered up their papers, handed them back to the boys, and zapped them right back home again.

In the living room, my mom and dad were holding hands and staring at a corner of the room. They didn't turn around to say hello, and I understood that they were working together on a spell and that they couldn't break their concentration.

Things were looking really serious. A terrified-looking Tom was hunkered down by himself in the corner, where Mom and Dad were staring. The air was shimmering all around him and the bright daylight of the room was flickering. There was a deep, deep hum that seemed to be getting louder and louder.

Munch nudged up against me and I put my arm around him because I could tell he was getting scared. Heck, I was a little scared myself because my parents looked so serious.

We all stared at Tom, who crouched down with his tail all big and puffy. Did you know when cats are scared, their tails puff up to make them look bigger to whatever is threatening them? In this case of course, it wasn't much of a defense because poor Tom still wasn't much bigger than a handful. I actually felt sorry for him for even trying, but I guess it's cat instinct and he couldn't help it.

Just then, *WHAM!!* The room went totally dark, even though it was only three o'clock in the afternoon. That deep hum grew so loud that Munch and I had to let go of each other to cover our ears.

In the corner, a little light appeared, right down where Tom was cowering, and it got bigger and brighter until the whole room filled with light— and in one great, bright flash, Tom, the thirteen-year-old boy, stood there.

He looked absolutely delighted to be a boy again and he opened his mouth to speak . . . But before he could say a word, the room went black again and there was all sorts of scary crashing and thumping. Then the daylight returned and the hum stopped abruptly.

Tom was back to being a little kitten, my parents looked wrung out and exhausted, and the room was a wreck. All the chairs were overturned and most of the books and ornaments had fallen off shelves.

"Whoever did this had powerful skills," muttered my dad. "I'd better talk to March Hall again." And he headed off to Mom's office.

My mom shook her head sadly and came over to give Munch and me a hug.

"Kids, don't you worry. We'll find a way to help Tom somehow. In the meantime, you're going to need to spend a lot of time with him to keep him company and to let him know that you understand what's going on with him."

I picked Tom up and cuddled him, whispering that it was all going to be okay. Then I took him up to my room.

"Hey, I know what will make you feel better," I said. "You can sit here on my shoulder and read my science textbook while I study for my science test."

It made things a little difficult actually, because he was such a fast reader that he kept leaping down into my lap to try to turn the page before I was ready. Finally, though it took a while, we worked out a rhythm. I opened up my ancient civilizations book on the table beside me so that he could read that while he waited for me to finish the page in the science book on my lap.

At this point, I didn't know who this kid Tom was, but I could have told you one thing even then. He was smart.

CHAPTER 13

The March Hare Gets on My Nerves

A few weeks went by with my parents still worrying a lot and staying up late working on spells and potions and doing lots and lots of research. No matter what they tried on him though, Tom was still a cat.

Dr. March Hall came over practically every single night to confer with my folks. Whenever Tom was in the room with them, I happened to notice that the doctor always sat as far away from him as possible. It seemed funny to me, but when I asked Mom what she thought about it, she said that he was probably allergic. A lot of people are, you know. Glad I'm not.

It got to be no fun at all around the house at dinnertime because it felt like the March Hare, excuse me, I mean Dr. March Hall, was there all the time and he wasn't what you could call a really fun guy. First of all, he talked to Mom and Dad in this kind of snooty, I'm-smarter-than-you tone and he never talked to Munch, or Tom, or me at all, as if we were too unimportant to even notice.

My mom doesn't like it when adults don't treat kids with respect, and I could see Dr. March Hall's attitude toward us was bothering her, but he was never actually rude, so she couldn't really say anything. Instead, she was just extra nice to us.

One night, Munch went a little over the top at dinner and tried to levitate the butter, which he doesn't really know how to do yet. He ended up knocking it into his glass and spilling his milk into the doctor's lap. You could tell that Dr. March Hall was deeply annoyed, but Mom didn't even reprimand Munch. She just zapped up the milk off Dr. March Hall's suit with a clean-up spell and gave the anxious Munch a big kiss, telling him not to worry about it because accidents happen.

Dr. March Hall looked sour for a minute and then he went back to droning on about ". . . multitiered stratum hexes with supplementary characteristics . . ." or something incredibly boring like that. Munch and I excused ourselves as soon as we could and went up to our rooms.

Whenever Dr. March Hall was there for dinner,

which as I've mentioned, was practically every night,
Munch and I never got to talk at all about drama club,
or music, or anything fun. Tom steered clear of Dr.
March Hall entirely, unless my dad picked him up
to try some spell that the doctor had recommended.
Once I even heard Tom hiss when the doctor arrived.
I knew how he felt.

Apparently, Tom's enchantment involved some
interlocking spells and security hexes that made it
very difficult for any counterspell of my mom and
dad's to get through. No matter what spell they tried,
it came up against a sort of magical firewall that
blocked them from going any further.

Even though I never got to talk about it at dinner
anymore, the play rehearsals were going really well. I
don't know if I was just doing some pretty good acting or what, but after we'd rehearsed a lot, I started to
feel as if I really was a kid who didn't believe in magic
and that Calvin and Dennis really were a funny talking mushroom and caterpillar.

I forgot all about my dangly hands, too, and I'm not
sure, but I think they stopped dangling and started
to look sort of natural. That is, I hope so. Anyway, at
least I didn't worry about them anymore. I have to say,
it was the most fun I ever had without using magic

and I couldn't wait until we got to perform the play in front of people.

Until then, at least I got to do it in front of Tom every night. He'd sit up on my dresser and watch me practice all my lines. One night, when I got a little lazy and didn't feel like practicing, he sat on the dresser anyway and stared at me, until I felt guilty enough to run through them one time before bed.

I was sort of sorry about my costume though. I had been hoping for something really showy and glamorous like the kind of thing that Aunt Sophie got to wear in the Civil War movie. Unfortunately, all I got to wear was pajamas because my character was supposed to have fallen asleep while reading. Mom had a great idea though. She got me just some plain flannel pajamas and then she zapped pictures of books all over them. And then, just as a private thing between us, she made them all my favorite books like *The Tale of Despereaux* and the Lemony Snickets and the *Chronicles of Narnia* and Harry Potter. I mean honestly, could my costume be more perfect?

CHAPTER 14

Tom Gets Depressed

Back at home, I'd been noticing that Tom, who despite being about four weeks older than when we first got him, was still just as tiny as he was to start with. Dad told me that's a built-in fail-safe for *involuntary* morphing spells, which told him that Tom didn't ask to be morphed. Somebody did it to him—how awful is that?

Anyway, this fail-safe is apparently built into magic code. This is something I haven't gotten to yet in my Witch Studies (and yes, I am a little behind with them, but only because Miss Linegar is a homework fiend).

The fail-safe is so that no matter how long enchanted people are out of their normal shapes, they can return to their lives in exactly the same moment they left it without being any older. Once Mom and Dad got Tom back to human and figured out exactly where and when he lived, they'd easily be able to zap him back to within a moment or two of when he got zapped out. Then time would shift and his mom and dad wouldn't be aware that they had ever been worried sick about him being gone. Still, that didn't mean that in the time line that was going on right now they weren't worried to death, or that if Mom and Dad couldn't find a way to reverse the spell, his parents might *never* get Tom back.

I know that whole time line business is really hard to follow. Dad assures me it will all get clear by the time I'm in Witch University, but for now it tends to give me a big headache. Let's just say, if Tom gets changed back to a boy, everything will work out fine but if he doesn't, there's some family back in the nineteenth century (yes Miss Linegar, I know that's the 1800s) that is going to be pretty sad.

Speaking of Tom, he'd started to seem a little depressed. I kept handing him books off of all the shelves in the house because that usually made him get excited, but he had no interest in a lot of the stuff that I really liked, except for history and my dad's *Complete Works of Shakespeare*. When I was going through my books, trying to find him new things to read, I realized he'd already been through all the science books in the house. Every single one I picked up had grubby little paw marks all over each page.

I started going to the library to get science books, which kind of confused Mrs. Koneff, the librarian, because she'd never seen me borrow anything but fiction before. I decided it was better not to try to explain.

Anyway, I'd come home with the books and Tom and I would cuddle up and read every night. After that he began to cheer up. And even though he mostly liked to spend his time reading, he'd even chase a few paper balls around now and then, when Munch fired them out of his toy cannon for him.

Mom and Dad were still trying new spells on him every day without much luck. The best that happened was that sometimes we'd see Tom flicker into boyness again, for just a moment or two. Is "boyness" a word, or did I just make it up?

One day, when I came home from the library with an armload of books for Tom, something really weird happened. I heard a voice *inside* my head. It was so strange and unexpected that goose bumps flared up and down my arms, and the back of my neck prickled as if all my hair was standing on end. If I'd been a cat, my tail would have been huge.

When you're a witch, you're used to strange occurrences, but you can usually count on your own head as being a private place. I mean, come on! People aren't supposed to suddenly start talking inside of it. How'd you like to be innocently walking in the door one day with an armload of books for your kitten and hear this in your head: *"Father's going to owe me a lot of dimes soon"*? How random and creepy is that???? What does something like that even mean???

I mean, I'm used to hearing my own voice in my head, but this was a *boy* voice, for heaven's sake. It certainly didn't belong inside *my* head. I was so startled that I dropped my books and started screaming for Mom, who came tearing out from her office. I made such a racket that Munch, who was watching his hour allotment of Saturday morning cartoons in the living room, let out a yell and zapped himself right into the TV. Poor little Tom jumped about a mile, into the pocket of my dad's jacket that was hanging on the coatrack near the front doorway.

I threw myself into Mom's arms and tried to tell her about what was frightening me so badly and then I heard the voice again.

"Crikey! What's Abbie so fired up about? You might think the barn was burning down!"

I mean, that's even creepier than the remark about

the dimes because my *name* was involved, and I got scared all over again and the goose bumps got even bigger. I jumped around as skittish as a squirrel and my mom had a terrible time getting me to calm down enough to tell her what had just happened.

As soon as I managed to tell Mom what I'd heard in my head, she zapped Dad right out of his office without even calling him first. He had a stethoscope in his ears and he looked a little peeved until he saw how upset everybody was. Mom explained what had happened and he got that worried look we'd seen so often lately and put his hand on my forehead and started muttering incantations.

Just then, Tom popped up out of the jacket pocket on the coatrack and jumped onto Dad's shoulder. I heard the voice again.

"Blame it! I wish he'd speak a little louder."

Then, with a slow, dawning realization, I understood that it was *Tom's* voice I was hearing.

Knowing that, I felt a lot better because I knew that Tom loved me and would never do anything to hurt me. I told Mom and Dad what I'd figured out and they looked very relieved too. They started talking and came to the conclusion that some of their de-enchantment spells must have broken through part of the communications barrier that Tom was hexed with.

"Tildy. Do you think we ought to call in March Hall?" asked Dad.

Thankfully Mom answered, "Well, we don't have much to go on yet, love. So we might as well wait to see if anything else happens first."

Well hurray. Maybe we could have one dinner where Munch and I got to squeeze in a few words.

"At least we know we're making progress," added my mom, giving me and Tom a comforting pat. Then she went into the living room to zap Munch out of the TV, where he was having a great time, running around behind Sylvester as he chased Tweety Bird.

Suffering succotash. I like the old cartoons the best, don't you?

CHAPTER 15

I Get into Very Big Trouble

I tried all that night to have a conversation with Tom. Though he always seemed to understand what I said, sometimes, if he wasn't looking right at me, he didn't seem to hear me at all. Meanwhile, his own voice kept breaking through to me now and then.

It wasn't as if Tom was able to hold a real conversation with me, but just as if I got random glimpses into his mind. Though some of his thoughts were really clear, like the father and the dime remark (which still *creeps* me out), a lot of them seemed scientific and technical and I couldn't understand what they were about. That was one busy mind.

There were really a lot of thoughts about telegraphs, which was a way they used to communicate in the days before phones and e-mails and texting, when they'd tap out a code over wires. Tom seemed to spend a lot of time thinking about them.

Sometimes I could sense a sadness coming from Tom and got images of a woman and a man and a whole bunch of kids who all seemed older than him. I figured this had to be his family, and whenever his thoughts of them popped into my head, I made sure that I was especially nice to him.

On the next Monday, I got a great idea. Knowing that Tom was incredibly smart and curious, I thought that he'd enjoy going to school with me. It might not be his grade level because I knew he was older than I was and knew a lot more, but I figured it would probably be more interesting than hanging around alone all day.

"But, Tom buddy. If this is going to work, you're going to have to behave and stay really still and quiet all day," I warned him.

Feeling like a spy smuggling secret documents, I snuck Tom into my coat pocket and Munch and I headed off to school. Munch loved the idea of having a secret like this and kept zapping cat treats into my pockets for Tom. When I discovered that one of the treats he popped in was a *sardine,* I had to ask him to stop. I almost made myself late for school again because I had to take the time to transfer Tom to my other pocket and zap in the disinfectant wave I'd recently learned from Dad to get rid of the fishy smell. Munch meant well though.

Of course I wanted Callie to know who I had with me, but I knew Miss Linegar wouldn't be exactly supportive of me bringing a kitten to school. So I took a moment as we were lining up outside the classroom to go in, to open up my coat pocket.

"Hey Callie," I whispered. "Take a look."

I felt the usual rush of wanting to share the whole truth with Callie because I knew she'd get a big kick out of the fact that I brought Tom so he could brush up on his schooling. It was okay though because Callie didn't ask for any explanations. She just looked amazed at my nerve and then giggled and slipped her hand into my pocket to stroke Tom's little head. She didn't even seem to wonder why I brought him, because she just thought it was so much fun to have Tom (or Benjamin, as she still thought of him) at school.

As we waited for the bell to ring, Callie whispered, "I'll stand in front of you by the closet, so you can hang up your coat and get Benjamin out of your pocket."

The plan worked perfectly. I hung up my coat in the coat closet, hid Tom under a book on the way to my desk, and then transferred him to my lap once I was sitting down.

Once I was in my seat, I whispered, "Remember, Tom buddy, just listen quietly and be very careful to stay under the desk."

Over at the next desk, I could see Callie biting her lips and trying not to giggle as Tom snuggled down in my lap. Meanwhile, I looked as studious and serious as I possibly could, in order not to attract Miss Linegar's attention.

We got through roll call with no problem and when we moved onto the "Drop Everything and Read" portion of the morning (I was reading *Harriet the Spy*), Tom fell right asleep. I knew he'd be interested when we got to science though, so when Miss Linegar told us to take out our science books, I gave him a little nudge.

"Please turn to chapter thirteen, the chapter on sound waves," Miss Linegar announced.

Well. I thought Tom would leap right up onto the desk, he got so interested. I had to keep petting him to calm him down, but it was hard not to laugh because he kept trying to crane one of his little pointed ears up above the desk. If Miss Linegar had happened to turn around, which thankfully she didn't, she would have seen a velvety little triangle of fur pointing straight at her and quivering with excitement.

Callie spotted it though and she turned red in the face from trying not to laugh. Right away, we both got the giggles so bad that it turned into one of those whispery, snorty moments when you try to stifle yourself even though your shoulders are shaking and tears start rolling down your face. Calvin and Dennis, who sat right in front of us, turned around curiously. I managed to shove Tom down where they couldn't spot him, and Callie and I both bit our lips really hard to stop our laughing.

That's a handy trick, by the way, that lip-biting thing to stifle laughing. Although, once Callie made me laugh so hard in assembly that my lip hurt afterward for hours. It was because of a little impersonation she sometimes does of Principal Oh, but that's another story.

Miss Linegar happened to sneeze, and turned away from the blackboard to get a tissue, but by then we'd gotten ourselves under control and she didn't notice us.

As I was trying to listen to the lesson and make notes, inside my head I kept getting rammed by sudden bursts of thoughts from Tom. The most frequent ones seemed to be *"Well, confound it! Tell us why, woman!"* and *"Can't you explain?"*

I saw that he was taking in the whole lesson, but it seemed as if his mind was racing ahead to try to figure out higher levels of what Miss Linegar was talking about. He was getting so frustrated at not being able to ask questions that he started to dance around in my lap and kicked into total hyper mode.

Finally, though I was doing all I could to keep Tom's head down and keep him quiet, he forgot about everything I'd told him and suddenly jumped right up on my desk.

"MEEEOOWWW!!!" he yowled . . . at the top of his lungs.

Well. So much for Tom's school career and so much for mine (almost). Now, I don't know how she expected *me* to know about it, but it turned out that Miss Linegar (who I *had* noticed was sniffling and sneezing quite a bit) is violently allergic to cats. When she heard the yowl, she jumped right onto the top of her desk. This would have been kind of funny, if a person didn't happen to be paralyzed with horror at the time—which believe me, I was.

Everybody in the whole class turned to look at

me, except for Callie, who had her face buried in her hands. Sympathizing once again.

Instantly realizing that he'd just bought me a whole peck of trouble, Tom stopped dead. I got the distinct impression that he knew a little something about problems with teachers.

I could tell Tom was remorseful, but his being sorry wasn't much help to me in facing the wrath of the red-faced and furious Miss Linegar, who was trying to regain her dignity as she slid down heavily off of her desk. She kept my doom pretty simple. Just a few short words.

She straightened her skirt. "Abbie," she said. (And she took a deep sniffly breath to maintain her self-control.) "Go to the principal's office . . . and take your *cat* with you."

CHAPTER 16

Three-Time Loser

Are there any worse words in the English language than those?

"Go to the principal's office."

Just five little words, none of them more than three syllables, but they pack a wallop, like the time Munch misjudged his baseball swing and hit me right in the belly.

"Go to the principal's office."

I kept hearing the phrase, echoing in my head, as I tucked Tom into my arms, got up from my seat, and made the long, long walk down the aisle of desks to the door at the back.

"Go. Go. Go. To the principal's principal's principal's office office office."

It was like everyone in class had turned to stone. Nobody moved and nobody made a sound. I tried to get out quickly, but the back door was locked like it always is, to catch and destroy the tardy, so I had to wrestle with it before I could get it open. As I closed it quietly behind me, I could hear a massive sneeze from the front of the room.

"RRRAAAACHOOOO!!!"

I don't know what she was so upset about. It's not as if *she* had to worry about hitting the ceiling.

I walked across the quiet yard on the way to the office and I added up the number of times I'd been sent to the principal so far this year. Yep. This made three.

The first time was completely Munch's fault though. I had spotted him through my classroom window, morphing himself into a basketball during his PE class . . . right in front of nineteen startled first graders and a shocked Mr. Merkelson. It was happening so fast I didn't have time to throw a time freeze spell on my own class as I hurtled out the door to throw one on Munch's class.

Of course all Miss Linegar saw was that I suddenly bolted up out of my desk, overturning my chair as I rushed out the door. From her perspective, I then immediately ran right back into the room. In reality, of course, I had time-frozen Mr. Merkelson and his class, moved into a different time mode, and flown up in the air to retrieve Munch as he slam-dunked himself into the hoop. Then I unmorphed Munch, gave him a serious talking to about not forgetting himself, and went through the usual rigmarole of casting forgetting spells and so on.

When I got back to my classroom, I realized, with a sudden, sick pang in my stomach, that I had neglected to cover myself there. I was forced to pick up my chair from where it was lying on its side and suffer through Miss Linegar's icy query.

"Young lady, do you find it amusing to disrupt the entire class?"

What made it particularly upsetting was that I couldn't think of a single thing that might acceptably explain suddenly jumping up, overturning my chair in my hurry to get out the door, and then returning in what seemed to be an instant. So I was stuck with letting Miss Linegar think that I found it "amusing."

That's when I heard those five little words for the first time this year.

"Go to the principal's office."

I got a note sent home that time, but luckily Mom and Dad understood, although Mom gave me a stern talking to about how fast a witch's reflexes have to be and how mine weren't getting any faster by skipping my spell technique practice.

I was all the way across the yard now and heading into the office. I could see the office ladies chatting back and forth as they worked, just as if this was a perfectly normal, nice day and not potentially the worst day of a person's entire life.

The office ladies could tell by my face that I wasn't there for any happy reason, like to borrow the phone to call home because I had a raging fever, or severe vomiting. Nope, it was pretty clear by the bleak, death-like look on my face that I was there for my third visit to the principal so far this year. And it wasn't even Thanksgiving break yet.

Mrs. Carol, who's a really nice lady, looked at me sympathetically and didn't even bother to ask why I was there.

"Hi there, Abbie," she said. "Mrs. Oh is on the phone right now but she'll be able to see you in a moment."

She seemed a little startled to notice that I had a kitten with me, but Tom was on his best behavior (for all the good it did me *now*) and she chose not say anything about it.

While I sat there awaiting my fate, I reflected on

the last time I sat in that very seat, as I was waiting for Mrs. Oh after the cafeteria food-hurling incident.

Just so you know, that wasn't really my fault either, or at least not *all* my fault. Lunch had been chicken nuggets with baby carrots that day and I was sitting with these kids Frankie, a boy from my class, and Alioune, who's a fourth grader. I happened to notice that Munch, who had just taken his first few levitation lessons, had started sending his food flying up all around the room. One nugget was followed by a carrot, followed by another nugget, marching along like they were toy soldiers, eight feet up in the air.

I saw people's mouths drop open and some scared-looking kids were starting to jump up out of their seats. The cafeteria was too crowded and busy for me to be able to throw a wide enough time freeze to be sure that everyone would be inside of it. So I did the only thing I could think of at short notice. I started throwing *my* food up in the air too, hoping to knock down Munch's.

Frankie, who's one of those kids who can't tell when he's going too far, grabbed his lunch and Alioune's too, and threw them as high as he could and well–I guess about every one of the 250 kids on first lunch break joined in. Pretty soon most of those kids were covered in nuggets, low-fat milk, and squished carrots.

Mom was a little less understanding that time and reminded me of when she'd had to time freeze a whole stadium of people at a baseball game when she was my age. She'd had to bail out my aunt Sophie, who was seven and had flown thirty feet up out of her seat to catch a foul ball. I didn't think it was the right time to mention that Munch is probably a whole lot harder to handle than "sweet little Sophie" was, because I could tell there were already heavy consequences involving spell drills in the offing. I will admit that after this incident, I did get a whole lot better at mass freezings.

In Mrs. Oh's office, I could hear the scary sound of Mrs. Oh's phone going back in its cradle. A sour feeling hit my stomach.

I watched miserably as Mrs. Carol got up to go in to tell Mrs. Oh I was there to see her.

Soon I could hear Mrs. Carol softly whispering, "Abbie Adams has been sent to you *again.*"

This was followed by a heavy sigh from Mrs. Oh.

I felt a sigh of my own escape me as Mrs. Carol stepped out. She gave me a nice little reassuring smile that somehow didn't reassure me, and motioned me into Mrs. Oh's office.

A sad-eyed Tom looked up at me as I trudged the long twenty feet across the office to Mrs. Oh's door and reluctantly poked my head in.

There she was, sitting at her desk with an exhausted look on her face. The look turned a bit grim when she saw that I had a kitten with me.

"What is it *this* time, Abbie?" she said, with what I thought was an unnecessary emphasis on the word "this." You'd think I'd been in her office fifty times, instead of three.

As I got all the way in and stood in front of her desk, I faced the bleak truth that this time I had no one but myself to blame. Munch had been on his best behavior since his meltdown the other day, Frankie was still sitting back in our classroom, probably waving his arm around as usual, trying to be the first one to answer every single question, and Tom hadn't asked to be brought to school, it was *my* big idea.

Now listen. This is important. I want you to know that I do understand that the only right thing to do in these situations is to admit that you did something wrong, say you're sorry, and face the consequences. I've certainly been in trouble enough times to have learned that lesson very, very well. So I can't really explain what I did next.

Maybe it had something to do with the fact that my mom and dad had been so worried lately and I didn't want to bother them. I'd like to think that was part of the reason anyway. But if I'm really honest with myself, I'd have to admit that I just turned into a great big chicken and couldn't face up to that inevitable phone call home to my parents, which—it spells out very clearly in the student discipline guidelines they always make us sign on the first day of school—is what happens on the third visit to the principal.

I watched Mrs. Oh trying to look patient as her hand snaked over to my file, which Mrs. Carol had already efficiently placed on her desk. Any second, she'd be opening it to look up my parents' phone number. It made me feel so chicken that if I'd been Munch, I would have sprouted feathers and started flapping around the room.

At least I didn't do that, but what I did do wasn't a whole lot better. I just felt something get so tense and tight inside of my chest that it was as if I had no control over things at all. That magic buzz built up in my fingers to the point that they started to feel as if they were burning. I stuffed Tom into my sweater pocket so that I wouldn't shock him. Then, before I'd even had a chance to think about it, I did something I know

no witch should ever do—I performed completely unnecessary magic on an unsuspecting mortal for no
good reason but to get myself out of a consequence
that I absolutely deserved.

Zap!!! My hands snapped up as if they were operat-
ing without any sort of orders from my head and a
flash of magic exploded out of them that froze Mrs.
Oh in her seat. I snatched up my file, raced up behind
Mrs. Carol and the other ladies in the outer office and
froze them too, then slammed my file back into the
first filing cabinet drawer, which had been left open at
the *A*'s. As I rushed out the front door, I hissed and
whistled a Forgetting Spell and undid the time freeze
so that the ladies would go back to their day without
any recollection that I'd ever been there.

Without stopping to think for a second about what
I'd done, I just walked right off campus and took Tom
home.

I'll bet you're thinking I wished I went to a school
like Hogwarts where you could do magic all day long
without getting into trouble. And you're right, I do.
Even Professor McGonagall isn't nearly as strict as
Miss Linegar. But here's the problem. I don't go to
Hogwarts. And I'm not supposed to do what I did.

Nobody was home at my house, so I just let myself

in, got out a couple of cat treats for Tom, went upstairs to my room, and threw myself on the bed. It had been a really hard day, even if it was still only a little after 10 a.m., and I fell asleep on my bed with my head buried under the pillow.

CHAPTER 17

We Find Out Who Tom Is

When I woke up, though Mom and Dad still weren't home, I could hear the faint tap, tap, tap of computer keys.

I pulled myself up off my bed and went down into my mom's office to investigate. There was Tom, sitting right up on the keyboard of my mom's computer, tapping sort of slowly with his tiny right front paw and staring in awe at the computer screen. Munch and I aren't actually supposed to use that computer because my mom's got all the household accounts and her stuff for real estate school on it. I don't think she's that worried about *me* doing anything wrong, because fifth grade has computer class every Friday, but I figure she knows Munch well enough to realize she'd be risking her hard drive by letting him play with it. Just another example of how having a little brother can be a big pain.

I was already feeling guilty about everything and I didn't want anything else on my conscience, so I told Tom he'd better cut it out. He jumped about a foot into the air because I guess he'd been concentrating so hard he hadn't heard me come in. I took him in my arms and cuddled him and leaned over to look at what he'd been doing.

When I saw that he'd typed the name *Thomas Edison* a strange chill came over me.

Of course. Suddenly, everything started to make sense. Forgetting all about my mom's restrictions, I did a Google search on Thomas Edison as a boy and right away I was looking at some old-fashioned photos of the boy I had seen for just a second the first time I looked into my kitten's eyes.

Tom was so fascinated by what was on the computer, he kept jumping out of my arms onto the keyboard, causing the pages on the screen to delete, or to jump all over the place so that I couldn't read anything. Finally, I held him against my chest with my left hand and used my right hand to scroll through the information that came up.

From what I'd gotten to know about Tom the last

few weeks, I had no doubt at all that the hyper little kitten trying to squirm out of my grasp to jump down onto the keyboard right now was the famous Thomas Edison himself.

I learned a lot about him from the computer search. Did you know that Thomas Edison, who was one of the smartest guys ever and one of the most amazing inventors of all time, had teachers who didn't like the way he was always asking them questions they couldn't answer? They told his parents he was thick-headed and hyperactive. I guess teachers weren't always so understanding back in the old days either. Are you listening, Miss Linegar??? Anyway, Tom's mom, who *knew* he wasn't thick-headed, took him out of school and taught him herself.

I was amazed to see how correct a lot of my impressions were about Tom. Just as I thought from some of the images I got, Thomas Edison was the youngest in a big family. I even figured out that first creepy statement I heard in my head about the dimes. It seems that Thomas's dad used to pay him a dime for every book he read.

Tom made so much money from all those dimes that he started his own little business selling snacks on a commuter train, even though he was still a young kid. He used the money he made from *that* to buy equipment to do scientific experiments, and once he actually burned down his dad's barn with an experiment that went bad.

As I got to the part about the barn fire though, Tom suddenly buried his furry little face against my chest as if he were really upset. I had been reading out loud but I stopped as soon as I realized what was written there. Listen to this. It seems Tom's dad publicly *thrashed* him for burning down the barn.

Fast as I could, I scrolled down a couple of pages of information and I could see that Tom was relieved to skip over that part. I was still a little shook up though, to have read it.

Gee. I'd just been thinking how great Tom's dad was with the dime thing and everything and then he goes and *thrashes* Tom . . . beats him, in front of other people even. I bet his mom didn't like that Tom got thrashed. There's no way my mom would let something like that happen. Not that my dad would ever dream of it.

Now, I guess you probably know that Edison perfected the long-burning lightbulb, but did you know he invented the first recording device too? No wonder he got so excited when he heard my CD player, he'd never heard recorded music before. It wasn't invented in his day, because he hadn't invented it yet.

Edison also invented the first motion picture . . . the first movie. How's that for something amazing? Or, did you know that he worked running a telegraph machine when he was young and knew Morse code and everything?

Oh, listen to this. This is funny. I guess Tom had the night shift at the telegraph office and he was supposed to telegraph a message in to his boss every now and then, so that his boss would know he was paying attention to the job. But Tom invented a way for his check-in message to go in automatically, so that he could spend his time reading and doing experiments. And it worked great too—until the night his boss dropped in and found out that Tom wasn't even in the office. Ooops.

That reminds me of the time last year when Munch tried to send a duplicate of himself to school so he could hide out and play in his room. The spell was a little too hard for a kindergarten witch though, and when the duplicate walked into the kitchen for break-fast . . . Well . . . Let's just say that Mom had no problem figuring out that a two-foot tall kid with no ears wasn't Munch.

As I looked down at Tom, focusing with absolute attention on the computer screen, I realized that the story about the telegraph office was new to him too. That incident happened later in his life when he was well into his teens, and he was only about thirteen now. In fact, Tom seemed pretty surprised by that telegraph story.

He sure was interested in reading this biography of himself though, and I thought about how fantastic it would be to be able to read about what sort of things I was going to do when I grew up. Problem is though, if we couldn't get Tom back soon, none of this was going to happen, and within a year or two, if we logged onto the computer to look him up, we weren't going to find any mention of him at all. Who knows if we'd even have computers?

I don't know much about the math of time travel, but according to my parents, there's always a little lag time before some change in the past affects the future. If there wasn't some leeway in the time line like that, there'd be laws against witches going back at all. We're supposed to leave everything exactly as we found it and not make our presence known, which is why I have to do stuff like pose as a pillar. Every now and then though, you get a rogue witch who goes back and tries to make things different. It was starting to look as if Tom may have had the bad luck to run up against one of those witches.

The more I read about Tom, the more I felt as if we had a lot of things in common . . . well, except maybe for that genius inventor thing. He was misunderstood at school and he got in trouble all over the place just like I do. Except for the fact that my main trouble is magic and his was his amazing brain, our childhoods seemed to have a lot in common. Um, not including that thrashing business, which made me pretty glad that I'm a twenty-first-century kid, where that kind of thing is frowned on.

As I read more, something else got explained to me too about how sometimes Tom didn't seem to hear me unless he was looking right at me. This is really sad but it seems Tom was pretty deaf as a kid and got even deafer as an adult. Some people think this made it easier for him to think so clearly, because he had fewer distractions.

It makes sense to me, especially when I think about those times when I'm trying to read, while Munch pretends to be a rock star and conjures up the sound of a roaring crowd. Just try concentrating on a boring spell technique chapter when somebody in the next room keeps screaming, "For those about to rock, we salute you!" over the sound of thousands of screaming fans.

Actually, Munch has a little bit of a lisp, so when he says it, it's more like "For thoth about to rock, we thalute you!"

Okay, I admit it, it's cute.

Tom and I spent the rest of morning in front of the computer and when my mom came home at lunchtime, we were still at it. At first she got that kind of tired-looking expression she gets when she sees me doing something she's asked me not to do (not that I do it all that often . . . well, not if I can help it). Her expression changed quickly though when I told her I had found out who Tom was.

CHAPTER 18

Egg on My Face

Well, Mom got on the phone to Dad right away and he zapped home to talk about it.

Apparently, once the enchanted person's identity is known, there's a lot that can be done about tailoring a spell to free them. In fact, Dad got so excited that he kept accidentally levitating up a few feet into the air. Mom had to yank him down by his doctor's coat, so she could talk to him eye to eye.

Once Dad calmed down enough, he picked up Tom and brought him really close to his face. It was funny, but I almost started to cry when he looked straight into Tom's eyes.

"It's a very great honor to meet you," he whispered. "And I promise you that we will do everything in our power to get you safely home to your family."

You know, I hadn't thought about it, because a big

part of me still thought of Tom as my fuzzy little pet, but I guess it really was an honor to have Thomas Edison staying at my house. I hoped we'd be able to start communicating better soon so I could see what it was like to have a genius for a friend. I mean, when you're a witch, you get to see a lot of famous types and to listen to them, but it's not often that you actually get a chance to get to hang out with them and be buddies.

So. Let me ask you this. Have you ever been in class and the teacher asks a question and you get all excited because you know the answer? You wave your hand in big, huge circles trying to be the one who waves it hard enough to get called on. Inside, you're going, "Me! Me! Ask me!" because it feels so good to have the answer and you just can't wait to be the one to say it. Well, all of a sudden, that's exactly how I felt because I had an absolutely *brilliant* idea. It was the solution to the entire Tom problem.

Being very modest as you know, I tried to downplay it a bit, because when you suddenly realize that you are possibly the smartest kid on the entire planet, witch or human . . . you try to act a little humble, so as not to look big-headed or anything.

"Mom," I said very quietly, taking a deep breath before I continued. "Tom knows how to use the

computer now. He can type out the name of whoever
ENCHANTED HIM!!!"

Okay, maybe I didn't manage to look quite as
humble as I'd hoped, because by the time I'd finished that sentence, I was yelling at the top of my
lungs and jumping up and down and grinning from
ear to ear and . . . well . . . okay, I'll confess. I ran
around the room yelling, "I'M A GENIUS!!! I'M A
GENIUS!!!"

Mom and Dad let me run around for a moment
or two and then Mom said, "Abbie, sweetheart.
You're certainly a very bright girl, and we're all aw-
fully proud of you. However, it's clear to me that you
are way, way behind in your Witch Studies and we
are definitely going to have to do something about
that."

Ouch. I felt like I was a big balloon that somebody
popped a pin into. So I thought hard . . . and then I
thought harder . . . and then with a sinking feeling in
my stomach, I finally recalled . . . that way back in the
third-grade textbook on enchantments and spells . . .
oh yeah . . . There was a whole section that explained
that forced enchantments always come along with a
companion spell. And guess what that spell does. It
stops the enchanted person from being able to reveal

who was responsible for their enchantment. It's that communications barrier thing.

Ooops.

Do you know that expression "Egg on your face"?

I had a *dozen* eggs on mine.

Mom and Dad started dragging heavy volumes out of their spell library in the basement and piling them up in the living room. Tom continued tap-tap-tapping on the computer because, after watching me, he knew how to surf the Internet. He was doing Google searches on everything imaginable, while I made peanut butter sandwiches for everybody. Well, except for Tom, who seemed to prefer cat food despite having started off as a human.

And it wasn't until we actually sat down to eat that my mom suddenly got a really startled look on her face as if something had just occurred to her. She turned to me.

"Abbie. What on earth are you doing home from school in the middle of the day?"

The bite of sandwich I'd just wolfed down so happily felt as if it had turned into a big lump of cement in my stomach. My brain seemed to freeze so that not a single thought popped in. I know I must have looked as if somebody had zapped a paralysis spell on me, because I just sat there with my mouth hanging open.

Mom quietly put her sandwich back down on the plate and took a slow breath. "It's all right, Abbie. You can tell me," she said.

But I couldn't. I just couldn't. Hey, don't get me wrong, my mom's a very understanding person. I think she'd be okay about the fact that I broke school rules and brought Tom to class because I was trying to do something nice for him. Even the fact that I got sent to Principal Oh for the *third* time this year might be all right because that was about Tom too. Still, I was pretty certain that she was going to have a really, really hard time accepting that I did something as selfish and immature as casting a spell on unsuspecting people: not to protect my little brother, not to keep my witchiness a secret, and not to help anyone else, but to just save myself from a consequence that I pretty much deserved.

I knew she'd be really disappointed in me, because I was disappointed in myself. And I hate disappointing my mom.

And so what did I do? Did I tell the truth and let my mom know what a big jerk I'd been? Did I make things better by accepting responsibility for my mistake and facing up to whatever consequences there might be?

Uh. No.

I made things about a million times worse by doing something I'd always sworn I would never do. I lied to my mom.

"Oh yeah," I said. "I didn't feel well at all when I got to school. Queasy, you know? But then I came home and took a big nap and I felt much better."

"Strange that I didn't get a call," said my mom, looking annoyed that the school would just send me home without letting her know.

She put her hand on my forehead and you know what? I was so flushed and uncomfortable about all the horrible lies I'd just told that I actually felt hot to her. So she gave me an aspirin and tucked me back into bed.

If you think you might ever feel bad about lying to your mom, try lying to a mom who fusses over you with cool cloths on your head and serves you pineapple juice and brings a TV into your room, to turn on your favorite TV show, even though it's not a TV day, and brushes back your hair from your forehead to give you kisses. You don't even know how bad bad can feel, until then.

CHAPTER 19

It All Catches Up with Me

Even though I was feeling so guilty, I ended up having a really nice afternoon because the old *Willie Wonka and the Chocolate Factory* was playing on the classic channel. Isn't it a funny thing about a really great movie or book? You could be having the worst day ever but while your mind gets involved with Charlie and his grandpa's troubles, you forget about your own. I lost track of the time completely.

Dad was busy with Tom and the disenchantment spells, and I was all snuggled up in my bed in front of the TV, happily engrossed in watching Willie Wonka dancing around with the Oompa-Loompas. Then, at 2:45, my mom walked out the front door to go get Munch at school . . . *and to pick up my homework from Miss Linegar!!!*

Well, I never found out *exactly* what happened

when my mom dropped by Miss Linegar's classroom. I figure she probably went in there pretty cheerfully and asked Miss Linegar how she was. Maybe she said something about how I was feeling much better and that I'd be at school tomorrow. I'm not sure that's how it went, but I did get some information later from Callie, who happened to be in the schoolyard, waiting for baseball practice, as my mom arrived.

Callie said that shortly after my mom walked into the bungalow, Miss Linegar came sailing out, with her hand on my mom's arm. Then she steered Mom right across the yard to the school office, at about eighty miles an hour.

In the office, I would guess that the office ladies—or Principal Oh—probably said that they hadn't seen me all day and didn't know that I'd been sent there in the first place.

Now, another mother might have assumed from the evidence that I'd chickened out of visiting the principal and gone straight home. But unfortunately, my mom can sense when there's been a spell recently cast and she could smell my time freeze/forgetting spell from about a mile away.

Willie Wonka was just winding up when I heard the front door close. There was a big whoosh of wind as Munch came swooping up into my room at top airspeed.

"Abbie, Abbie," he whispered. "Watch out. Mom's really mad."

My heart froze in my chest and it finally sank in that not thinking about what I did wasn't going to make it go away.

Munch wisely went zipping around the corner to his room so he could get the heck out of the way.

I sat bolt upright in bed, listening to the murmur of Mom and Dad talking downstairs. I'll bet you can guess the subject of their conversation. I got even more worried when they didn't come up right away, because that usually means that my mom is giving herself a little time-out, to cool off before she confronts us about something we've done. She seemed to be needing quite a bit of cooling off this time.

What had I been thinking? I mean, if I was going to do something as wrong as slapping a forgetting spell on a whole office full of people, you'd think it might have occurred to me that if I didn't want to get caught for it, I should slap one on the teacher who'd sent me to the office in the first place. Then I felt guilty for thinking that—because of course I shouldn't have been doing any hexing in the first place.

BOOM!!!

Suddenly the Schnitzler boys came crashing into my room, right out of thin air, fighting over a TV remote. It practically gave me a heart attack, since as you can imagine, I was in a very nervous state as it was. By now of course, I had the spell to send them home right at the tip of my fingers. After I recovered from my fright, I zapped them right back . . . just as my mom and dad came into the room looking very, very serious.

"Abbie," said my mom. "We need to talk."

From the look on my mom's face, I could tell that Munch had been wrong about her. She wasn't mad. No. It was much, much worse than that. She was surprised at me and very, very disappointed.

You know, it's a funny thing. I thought the disappointment would be the worst thing, but it turns out that her being *surprised* at my behavior was actually way worse. That's because it meant Mom had a whole different idea of how mature I was, an idea I really *liked* her to have, and now it was gone.

Dad was looking serious too. He sat in my desk chair. "So, Abbie Dab," he said. "Can you explain to us what happened at school?"

"I guess you know already," I said—hoping not to have to actually say it out loud.

"Well, honey, we've heard Miss Linegar's side of things, but now we'd like to hear yours," he said.

Mom was very quiet, but as I sat there all miserable and afraid to speak, she did something so unexpected and so great that it makes me cry just telling you about it right now.

She sat on my bed and she put her arms around me and she gave me a really, really big hug. And then I remembered something I'd always known but had forgotten about for just a while, that no matter what I did, how bad it was, or how poorly thought out, that my mom was always going to be on my side. And I started to cry . . . big-time . . . big huge sobs.

All the stuff I'd been keeping to myself all school year came gushing out of me like a river. I cried about how hard it was to keep my secret from Callie and how hard it was to cover up for Munch all the time and how Miss Linegar always seems to think the worst of me, and how worried I was about Tom and how sorry I felt for him and how really, *really* sorry I was for casting a spell on the ladies in the office.

My mom pulled me into her lap. "I thought something was wrong lately," she said.

She rocked me back and forth like I was still a baby, and you know what? I didn't mind that at all. And

Dad sat on the bed beside us and stroked my hair as I sobbed.

"Oh, my Abbie Dabbie Do," he said. "Everybody makes mistakes. It's all going to be okay."

This went on for a little while and I was just starting to feel like I could stop crying enough to start talking normally, when this big fly kept bumping up against my face. No matter how many times I brushed it away, it just kept coming back.

"Okay, Munch," I said. "I know it's you."

The fly puffed out into a worried-looking, curly-headed little boy and Dad pulled him down onto his lap so we could all snuggle up on the bed and talk.

Well, I won't tell you everything that was said but I'll just let you know that Mom and Dad started telling me stories about similar experiences they'd had as kids. They talked about mistakes they'd made and things they had done wrong.

"So sweetheart, you can see we know a little something about what you've been going through," finished my dad.

Don't think they let me off the hook about how wrong it was to do what I did. But they did manage to convince me that everything was going to be okay.

Of course I promised never to do anything like that

again, and especially not to lie to them, and I also promised to reread the chapters on witch etiquette in human/witch dealings . . . in all *four* basic witchy handbooks. I could tell Mom was thinking about asking me to write something about it. She does that sometimes, to make sure I understand something, but I guess, this time, she thought I was going through enough.

Whew.

Munch even promised to try to control his behavior better, so that I wouldn't have to cover up for him all the time.

Well, I guess I'll believe that when I see it.

Next morning before school, I went to visit Mrs. Oh (for the fourth time this year, but who's counting?). I was supposed to apologize for not coming to her office when Miss Linegar sent me there. Okay, that was a little bit of a lie because of course I *had* come to her office, but I could hardly apologize for casting a spell on her, could I? And anyway, in chapter one of the first Witch Handbook, which I read after dinner the night before, there's a whole page about how certain tiny lies *might* be necessary in dealings with humans. That's as long as they're only to cover up witchiness.

Might be necessary? Who are they kidding? Much

as I hate it, I've probably had to lie to Callie about a million and a half times.

Mrs. Oh told me that she and Miss Linegar had been discussing me and had decided that I'd have to be benched during recess, for a week. I'd also have to write an essay on how bringing pets to school can be a big distraction for the other students. Oh yeah, in the essay, I was also to mention how pets at school might bother people with allergies like . . . you know who.

Needless to say, as far as assigning me extra work, Miss Linegar had none of my mother's qualms about how much I'd been going through recently. In fact, I got the impression that Miss Linegar would have liked to do something more severe (big surprise), like suspend me from school. Thankfully, Mrs. Oh wasn't quite as strict. Hey, who is?

Finally, the last and most horribly uncomfortable thing I had to do was go see Miss Linegar herself, before class started.

I knocked on my classroom door at ten minutes to eight. I had to knock twice before she finally came to the door to unlock it, and then when she did, she just stood there silently with her arms folded across her chest. You know, some kids' teachers greet them with a cheery "Good morning!"

"Miss Linegar," I said, looking down at my sneakers. "I'm really, really sorry for bringing my kitten to school and I know I shouldn't have gone home without seeing Mrs. Oh and I'm really sorry about that too."

She didn't say anything.

I figured maybe something else was expected, so I thought a little harder. "I'm very sorry about your sneezes, too," I tried.

"Hmm," she said. "Well then, you'd better come in and get started on your essay."

And that was it. I wrote my essay, and then she made me write it again, ". . . In your best handwriting this time," and then the whole terrible incident was finally over.

But things weren't over for Tom. Not by a long shot.

CHAPTER 20

A Vermin-Free Home

When I got home, the Schnitzlers and Mr. Heatherhayes were sitting on my bedroom floor, playing cards and looking depressed. The boys were accusing each other of cheating. They kept throwing cards all over the place, while poor old Mr. Heatherhayes tried to keep peace by saying, "Now, now boys. Now, now boys," over and over.

I offered everybody something to drink but nobody seemed to want anything, so I zapped them all back home. Mom hadn't even known they were there because she'd been busy going through spell books in the kitchen while she zapped up dinner.

I got as depressed-looking as the Schnitzlers and Mr. Heatherhayes when I heard Dr. March Hall was coming over again. Now I couldn't even hang out with Mom because she'd be tied up, listening to stuffy old March Hare droning on and on and on.

It wasn't as if Dr. March Hall had actually been any help either. In fact, some of the counterspells he'd recommended had made things worse. Due to one of his bad ideas, I'd lost what little communication I had with Tom and never got his voice inside my head anymore.

Half the time we couldn't even find Tom when the doctor came over. He always seemed to be hiding under beds or inside closets with my mom's little book light and a pile of books.

Sometimes, while Tom was hiding, he performed small experiments. Once, when Mom and Dad sent me to find him, I hauled him out from under my parents' bed to find that all his hair was standing right on end. It seems he'd been rubbing his fur along the carpet doing an experiment on static electricity. When my hand touched him, there was a big *snap!!* We both got shocked and I nearly dropped him. His hair flattened right out after that though. It looked pretty funny.

At dinner, I happened to notice Tom sneaking in from the kitchen to slink under the dining room hutch behind old March Hare's seat. From there, I could see his big yellow eyes staring out. He was listening to the doctor, who was in the middle of a long, dull talk about "the thermodynamics of applied alchemical physics" and other subjects I had hoped not to have to suffer through . . . at least until I got to Witch University.

My mom and dad were trying to look interested, which almost required a special spell in itself, and Munch had fallen asleep in his peas. On the other hand, Tom looked fascinated (hey! I spelled it right) and snuck closer to Dr. March Hall's chair, cocking his little ears, trying to hear better.

Dr. March Hall kept his white hair pretty long and as I sat there beside him, I noticed that it started to rise up on the back of his neck, just like Tom's fur had risen in his static electricity experiment. All at once, the doctor turned around and STAMPED his foot really hard, almost crushing Tom. Tom just managed to leap out of the way in time, though he banged his poor little head against the hutch.

Tom went scampering out of the room as fast as his paws could carry him and Dr. March Hall turned back to my startled parents.

He seemed flustered for just a second but then he said something really rude. "I believe there was a filthy spider right behind my seat, Adams," he said. "And I must say, I'm surprised that witches with your family's status aren't able to keep their home vermin free."

I had to look up "vermin" after he left, which I'm happy to say was shortly after this event. The dictionary described it as "noxious, objectionable, or disgusting animals" and listed a bunch of examples, like flies, lice, bedbugs, cockroaches, and mice.

Well, if you ask me, a nice little household spider does not fit the definition of "vermin." Actually, I've spent quite a bit of time as a spider and once, at Witch Day Camp, I got the blue ribbon in a web-weaving competition.

There's nothing noxious or disgusting about spiders at all. In fact, they're some of the greatest creatures in the whole world and Munch thinks there's nothing as much fun as turning himself into one and sliding up and down on a silken thread.

All that's beside the point though, because you know what? I'm pretty sure there wasn't any spider behind Dr. March Hall's chair. I had the creepiest feeling that he somehow sensed Tom watching him and tried to stomp *Tom*!

Up in my room, under my pillow, with nothing but his tail sticking out, Tom was trembling all over. I took him onto my lap and wished that I could hear his thoughts the way I used to. Don't ask me why I felt this way, but I was pretty sure Tom would have something to tell me about Dr. March Hall that my parents would want to know.

I held Tom's furry little self up to my cheek and got a brief image of the teenaged boy who lived inside of him. That boy looked very worried and very sad.

After that, I had to go downstairs to help Dad with the dishes and . . . oh, I'll bet you've got to be wondering why witches would bother to do dishes when they could just zap them clean. Well, sadly, my mom has this theory that since we live in a non-witch world, she's going to have to teach us non-witch ways. And that, I'm very sorry to say, includes doing dishes and making beds and picking up toys and books and clothes off of bedroom floors. Sigh.

It's lucky for me that my mom's so busy and has to zap things herself pretty often, so just to be fair, she lets me zap my room clean and hex my bed to make itself at least *some* of the time. This wasn't one of those times though, and while she was picking peas out of a sleepy Munch's hair and putting him to bed, I had to do the dishes with Dad.

Now, my dad is not quite as strict as my mom with certain things, and after we'd washed and dried about half of the dishes, he grinned and said, "That's enough non-witchiness for one night, don't you think, Abbikins?" He wiggled his fingers at the rest of the mess, and the kitchen became sparkling clean, with everything nicely put away.

Even using magic, it would have been harder work for me than that. I'm embarrassed to admit, I would have had to chant for the washing, incant for the drying, and done a whole other finger-snapping hex for the putting away. For about the hundredth time that week, I promised myself to work harder on my spell technique.

Dad sat down on the window bench in the kitchen and slapped the seat beside him. I snuggled in next to him, which is something I've been doing since I was a little kid.

What I really like to do is lean against Dad's chest while he sings to me. He's got this big, deep voice and you can feel the vibrations of the sound in his chest when he sings. But he wasn't in a singing mood tonight.

Tonight he told me how sorry he was that we had to have Dr. March Hall over so often and how he missed hearing about my day while we had dinner.

I was really happy he brought up Dr. March Hall,

because I wanted to tell him how creepy I was finding him. Dad said that sometimes people just act badly and we can't control that. All we can control is how *we* react to it and try not to let it bother us.

"You know, Dabbs, at first, I got so annoyed about that 'vermin' remark that I had to hex my ears to keep them from smoking. But then I thought about how poor March Hall has never been able to sense what impact he's having on people. Why, he can't even tell how boring he is. Back in college, I used to have to zap myself with excess magic charge just to stay awake in his class. I had stings all over me. So I can hardly expect him to realize how rude his remark was, can I? After I thought about it that way, I actually felt a little sorry for him and I decided I might as well choose not to let his remark upset me."

Well, I wished I could have felt sorry for March Hare too . . . but I just didn't.

CHAPTER 21

It's Not All Bad Being a Witch

The next day was Saturday (FINALLY) and I got to sleep in late. Then I stayed in bed rereading Judy Blume's *Superfudge*. Every now and then, I like to take a look at it again just to remind myself that I'm not the only one with little brother troubles. Tom was snuggled up to me reading a twelfth-grade physics textbook Dad found in the basement. After a while, Mom called us to breakfast.

After we ate, Tom got right back to his book.

Mom said to Munch and me, "Kids, Daddy and I have been talking and we feel bad that we haven't had much time to do things together as a family lately. So, since Tom's doing okay for now, we've decided to leave him here for today, while we take a little break from figuring out how to reverse his enchantment." She smiled. "We have a special expedition planned."

Dad swooped in from the living room with a big grin on his face. "Oh magical offspring of ours," he announced, "we think that it's time to remind you about all the good things about being a witch." (He was looking directly at me as he said it.)

"So," he went on. "You will have to use your excellent young minds to guess what we are going to do today. I will kindly provide you with clues."

POOF!! He turned into a coconut.

"Oo, oo, I got it!" yelled Munch. (He loves this game.) "You're a rock! You're a rock! We're going to a rock concert!"

Then my dad popped back into human form. I could see that he and Mom were trying not to laugh at Munch's guess.

"Nope, I'm not a rock, buddy. Here, let's try this one," and then he turned into a palm tree.

"A palm tree! We're going to California to see Aunt Sophie," tried Munch, only not quite as excitedly because he really likes rock concerts. Once he nearly gave himself a concussion after he turned into a drumstick to get on stage with his favorite heavy metal band.

Dad popped back into human form again and said, "Good guess, buddy, but that's not it either. How about you, Abbie Dabbie?" and he turned into a pineapple.

"Hawaii?" I asked. I was really, really, really hoping that I was right because the last time we went to Hawaii, we went snorkeling, and snorkeling is one of my favorite things to do in the whole world.

"You got it," said Dad with a big grin. And in less time than it would have taken me to hex my bed to make itself, Mom and Dad had zapped us into bathing suits, Hawaiian shirts, and flip-flops and left extra food out for Tom. In the next moment, we found ourselves on Hanalei beach, on the Hawaiian island of Kauai.

It was beautiful there, with silky sand and bathtub-warm water. We spent half the time swimming and I even tried surfing, but the waves were really big. Surfing was so hard, I figured I'd really need a few days to get good at it and we had to go home that night, so I decided I'd save my strength and look for sand crabs instead. Plus I was getting tired of falling off and getting bonked by my board.

Munch didn't give up trying though until he got so tired that he couldn't get on top of the board at all. Dad fished him out and carried him back to shore.

Then we stepped out of sight of the other people on the beach and zapped to another place. It was a coral reef in a quiet little bay with no waves and you could put on snorkels and fins and swim around in the shallow, warm water seeing every kind and color of fish you could ever imagine.

Okay, so maybe it's not all bad being a witch. Munch was swimming around in front of me, pointing at all the fantastic colors of the fish he was spotting. Even though he's my annoying little brother and gets on my nerves a lot, there, drifting in that silent, watery world, with his curls floating around his head, he looked like one of those little Valentine's angels . . . that is until he turned himself into a great white shark and started chasing me.

CHAPTER 22

Things Get Scary

We ended a perfect day with fresh fish for dinner, Hawaiian shaved ices, and sweet milk from a straw, which was stuck right into a fresh coconut. By the time we all agreed we were ready to go home, Munch was asleep in Dad's arms, and Mom and Dad zapped us back.

Back at home, it was after midnight and I was looking forward to just toppling into bed. But when we materialized in our living room, suddenly I didn't feel tired at all. In fact, I felt as awake as if someone had thrown a bucket of cold water in my face. One look around showed that something was really, really wrong.

Furniture was upended, my mom's favorite vase was smashed on the floor beside the broken coffee table, and the carpet was pulled up. In the dining room, the hutch was dumped right over onto its face. Dad quickly zapped an invisible safety shield around us, laid the still sleeping Munch on the couch, and told me to wait there with him while he and Mom looked around the rest of the house.

I had a horrible, prickly feeling all over and I didn't want to let Mom and Dad out of my sight, but I knew I'd better stay there with Munch, in case he woke up and got scared. At this point, I think we were all too shocked to think straight.

From what Mom and Dad said, upstairs was just as bad as the first floor, with rooms tossed, drawers emptied, and bookcases overturned. All at once, I got a horrible, stabbing feeling in my heart as if somebody had just jabbed an icicle right through it.

"Mom! Mom!!" I screamed. "Where's Tom? Find Tom!!"

Mom gasped and she and Dad started calling Tom and carefully lifting up heavy furniture to make sure he wasn't crushed underneath anything.

I started calling to him too, and looking under things in the living room. "Tom!! Tom!!"

It didn't take long until all the noise woke Munch up. His eyes got big and round as he looked around at all the destruction. Without a word, he came over and stuck his hand in mine.

By now I was starting to feel sick with worry. After I looked everywhere I could think of downstairs, I hauled Munch up to the second floor to help look there. Mom and Dad were searching my room, and Munch and I ran into his.

Munch's room was a terrible mess, messier even than when Munch has had a friend over and they've played knights—and let me tell you, all that jousting and sword fighting and stuff . . . that gets messy.

All Munch's books were on the floor, his toy box was dumped out, and his bed was torn apart with the stuffed animals thrown all over the room. It was so scary, I almost started to cry.

I took a deep breath like Mom always tells me to do and tried to get quiet inside so that I could think clearly and come up with likely places that Tom might have hidden.

That's a human technique by the way, not a witchy one, that calming breath thing. FYI, it can come in handy.

Just then, Munch, who was already squeezing my hand really hard, tightened his clutch even more. With his other hand, he pointed off into the corner, where, underneath a lot of clothes and teddy bears, was his alligator hand puppet. . . . It was shaking all over.

Well, it could have been anything—some horrible spell cast on the puppet that was going to make it blow up if we touched it—or a hidden evil witch, shrunk down to miniature size and waiting to pop out at us—or even a possessed puppet that might start acting like a real alligator. So Munch and I didn't go near it but started screaming for Mom and Dad. They flew down the hall and got there in an instant. Then they leaped between us and the quaking thing in the corner.

As I've told you, Mom can sense magic and she quickly figured out that there was nothing bad about the puppet. So she and Dad gently picked it up . . . and pulled out a terrified, quaking Tom. His hearing isn't the best to begin with, and he'd been too muffled up in the puppet to hear our calls.

I don't mind admitting that now I did cry, great big gulping sobs. I was so happy to see Tom safe and not kidnapped or crushed or anything worse. His tail was huge and bushy and tiny shaky "mews" kept coming out of his trembling little mouth like he was trying to tell us how he felt. Now I cried even harder because I felt bad that *he* was scared. Mom and Dad passed him to me and I cuddled him and petted him until we both finally stopped shaking.

"Okay, kids. Everything's going to be okay now," said my mom comfortingly.

"Let's get back downstairs while we figure all this out," suggested my dad.

Mom and Dad put me and Munch and Tom on the couch in the living room under another safety shield, made absolutely sure there was nobody else still in the house, and then zapped the living room back to normal.

I was so happy to see everything back where it belonged instead of broken and tossed around on the floor that I decided from now on, I was really going to try to put things away when I was finished using them. Which by the way, Mom says she spends half her life trying to get me and Munch to do.

Munch conjured up a few sardines for Tom and I let him sit right in my lap to eat them even though they were horribly smelly. After that, he seemed to feel a lot better. Then, as if he'd suddenly remembered something, he leaped up out of my lap and bounded across the room to bump his head into my mom and dad, to get their attention.

Well, it was pretty obvious Tom had something to

tell them, and so they followed him into Mom's office, to where the computer still lay smashed on the floor. At the sight of this disaster, Tom's tail fluffed up huge and he started to shake again.

Mom zapped the computer back into shape, did one of those diagnostic things on it that you're supposed to do if you don't shut down the computer properly, and reassured Tom that no data had been lost.

Though it took a long time because he had to tap out everything with his little paw, one keystroke at a time, Tom opened a file that he'd clearly been working on just before the terrible events that wrecked our house began.

Boy, Tom was smart . . . and hardworking. I'd never known anybody like him. You know what he'd been doing while we were off drinking coconut milk and snorkeling around in Hawaii? He'd spent time with the spell books in the basement, then gone into all the witchy files on the computer and read up on the disenchantment spells he'd seen my mom and dad working on. Though Tom, of course, not being magical, couldn't cast any spells himself, he'd mixed and matched various spell and incantation formulas and had come up with a brand-new one for spell-breaking. It was something that my mom and dad (and by the way, neither of them is exactly understaffed in the brain department) had ever even thought of.

Dad got so excited, he immediately started puffing rainbow-colored smoke out of his ears and the only time I remember seeing him do that before was the day that Munch was born. (I wasn't very old but you know, that's the kind of thing you tend to remember.)

"Tildy, Tildy! Of course!" Dad yelled, grabbing my mom and hugging her. "All those lockbox spells we kept encountering partially opened up, over and over again, didn't they? But then, every single time, just as we were about to break through to the next level, they snapped shut so we were never able get through to the main enchantment. This formula—and Tom, may I say again, it's a great, great honor to know you—this formula provides a *time release* factor, so that each level will finally stay open long enough for us to get through to the next one. Time release! Time release! Of course. It's brilliant!"

Immediately, Mom and Dad started hauling advanced spell books and dusty old jars and bottles out of the basement and as Dad got to the top of the stairs, he turned back down to Mom and said, "Well, I guess I'd better summon up March Hall, since he's the big expert on this stuff and he'll want to oversee our formulations."

Well, quick as a sneeze, Dad suddenly went flying back down the stairs as if somebody had grabbed hold of his collar and hauled him down. Which is more or less what had happened, because my mom had done a little summoning of her own and had magically yanked him right back down to the basement so she could talk to him privately. Only, the thing is, she was so mad that she didn't manage to keep her voice quite as hushed as she meant to. So, upstairs, we could hear every single word she said.

And boy, she had a lot to say.

"Marley. I have had it with that big bag of hot air March Hall," she hissed. "The truth is, he hasn't done one single thing to help. In fact, if you would just think about it for a moment, you'd realize he's actually made things worse. And in any case, I am heartily sick of the sight of him. He's rude to the kids and he's full of himself and to be perfectly honest I would be very happy if he never darkened our door again!"

That's what she said, "darken our door." I like that expression, don't you? As if someone was so miserable and unlikable that their very arrival at your door sucked all the light out of the place. And hey, it certainly fit in Dr. March Hall's case.

Well anyway, after this extremely heated outburst from Mom, who never usually loses her temper at all, Munch and I stood at the basement door in stunned silence for a second.

Then we both said, at exactly the same time, "You go, Mom!!"

This sent us into a big fit of giggles and even got Mom and Dad laughing downstairs. Tom, however, had strangely dived right under the kitchen sink at the very moment that Dad had gotten hauled down the stairs. I guessed he was still pretty jumpy from his experiences earlier in the night.

CHAPTER 23

No More Kitten

Needless to say, Mom and Dad got busy with their formulations without the help of Dr. March Hall. As soon as they'd zapped the rest of the house back in order, I hauled Tom out from under the sink, so they could start applying some of the potions and disenchantment spells with the new formula that he had worked out.

Now that he'd gotten over whatever fright had sent him under the sink, Tom was remarkably calm and relaxed, as if he hadn't a doubt in his mind that his calculations were correct and were going to solve all his problems.

"Abbie," said my mom. "Your father and I think that this Time Release Disenchantment might work better if it were directed at Tom from three different angles. Do you think you'd be up to helping us out with this?"

"Would I ever!" I yelled, and shot up off the couch so she could teach me my part.

Mom and Dad were going to do the hard stuff but there was a tone that I had to hum while the Disenchantment Chants were recited, and I also got to sprinkle Tom with this glittery potion that smelled just like raspberries.

Mom and Dad started reciting and the air began to shimmer. The light in the room flickered and the magical hum got louder and louder, so that you couldn't even hear my hum anymore, even though I kept it up the whole time . . . well, except for when I ran out of breath for a second and remembered that there was a little spell I really ought to have cast to temporarily extend my lung power. I had a bad moment with that, but in the end, it didn't appear to matter.

This time, Tom seemed so unafraid that his tail didn't even puff up, though he did start to dance around excitedly.

Just like it had before when Mom and Dad got close to disenchanting him, a little light appeared around Tom and it got brighter and brighter until the whole room was bright as day. And then, just when the hum got so loud it was almost unbearable, it suddenly got absolutely quiet—and there was no more adorable little kitten—there was only Thomas Edison, thirteen-year-old boy.

Smoke, of course, began puffing out of my dad's ears, but it was pink and white this time as he rushed across the room to shake Tom's hand. My mom ran over too, and grabbed Tom and gave him a hug and Munch and I got over there fast and hugged him too. Then Dad seemed to change his mind about a handshake being quite enough under the circumstances, so he grabbed Tom and gave him a big hug as well.

"Success is sweet, Tildy!! Success is sweet!" crowed Dad as he turned around and gave my mom a huge hug too.

Tom stood a little stiffly, as if he wasn't all that familiar with getting hugged quite so much (we're big huggers in my family), but he was smiling and he took it all with very good cheer. He kept looking down at himself as if to make sure that he had human arms and legs again, instead of cat paws and fur. After a minute or two of this, he crossed to the mirror over the fireplace and then smiled happily at his face, as if it was an old friend he hadn't seen in a while. Which, in a manner of speaking, it was.

"Dr. and Mrs. Adams," he said with a formal little bow. "I'm mighty beholden to you both." And then he turned to me and his formal stance turned into an excited little shuffle. "And by jingo, Abbie, you've been bully, just bully getting me all those books!" Finally, he turned to Munch, who was feeling a little left out, I think. "And Munch, those sardines were grand, just grand. I can't thank you all enough for your kindness."

Munch liked that, so he conjured up another sardine then and there. Tom, though he did ask for a plate and a fork this time, seemed to enjoy it just as much as he had when he was a cat.

"Great Caesar's ghost," he said. "And to think there was a time that I didn't enjoy fish."

Even though it was about four o'clock in the morning now and we all should have been in bed ages ago, my mom flashed a little refresher spell on everyone and conjured up a chocolate cake and ice cream to celebrate. She even let Munch and me have soda, which is something she hardly ever does.

Once we'd eaten the cake and we'd laughed about how confident Tom had been that his idea would work, and after Dad had praised the brilliance of Tom's formula a few more times, things got serious. The excitement died down as we all sat together around the kitchen table.

"Now, Tom," said my dad quietly. "I think it's time you tell us what happened here tonight and more importantly to reveal who did this terrible, terrible thing to you."

You see, once an enchantment has finally been removed, all the accompanying spells that go along with it, like the one that stops people from revealing who their enchanter was, are gone too. It's a lucky little fact of witchy science.

Tom, who'd been hopping around excitedly, stopped dead and got an uncomfortable look on his face. "Oh blame it, Dr. and Mrs. Adams," he said. "I think p'raps you're not going to like what I tell you."

"No, no, Tom," said my mom. "We need to hear the truth and we need to hear it soon, so we can work on getting you back to your poor mother, who must be beside herself with worry."

At the mention of his mother, Tom overcame his reservations and broke the big news. His enchanter, the evil witch who, once caught, would never ever be allowed to practice magic again, was none other than, are you ready for this? *Dr. March Hall.*

Had you already guessed it? I hadn't. I guess there

were lots of clues but it just hadn't occurred to me that someone so impressed with himself could do anything criminal.

Well, my dad nearly fell off his chair he was so shocked, but my mom, though I don't think she had been exactly expecting it, didn't look completely surprised. I told you she was practically psychic, didn't I? And when I remember how angry she got about Dad's suggestion to bring the doctor in again, I think that she'd probably had a bad feeling about old March Hare for some time.

Tom told us a terrible story.

"It all feels like a rotten bad dream," he started, "because I hadn't any notion that anything horrid might happen that day. I'd just been doing a jolly little chemistry experiment in my home laboratory, when, from a clear blue sky, thunder boomed and black clouds burst in through the doors and windows. And by jingo, it made a power of racket.

"Everything went black and I couldn't even see my hand in front of my face," Tom went on, his legs bouncing up and down nervously as he leaned forward in his seat. "I tell you, it shot a scare right through me."

Now he leaped up out of his chair as if it was almost painful for him to sit still.

"I tried to run outside but I couldn't budge a lick," he continued. "Then, out of the darkness, came a bolt of lightning. As it cracked down right in front of me, frozen where I stood, Dr. March Hall appeared."

The terrified Tom had tried to call for his mom and dad but no sound would come out of his mouth, and his feet felt stuck to the floor. Worse yet (if you ask me), he'd had to stand there and listen while Dr. March Hall droned on and on self-importantly about his "ingenious" plan to step into Tom's place, claim his accomplishments for his own, and become the famous inventor that Tom was destined to be. Tom, of course, only being thirteen and not having even thought of perfecting the lightbulb or any of those things, didn't even know what Dr. March Hall was talking about.

"It all gave me a terrible turn," Tom said, "because 'twas clear that Dr. March Hall didn't mean me a bit of good. Until then, I hadn't any notion that alchemy was an honest science. Why, if any man had told me, I'd prob'ly have tried to lick him, but crikey!–I s'pose I've changed my mind since then!" And he threw back his head and laughed so hard, we all burst out laughing right along with him.

"I suppose you have!" roared my dad, jumping up

out of his chair and pounding him on the back.

"Well, the next thing that happened was that there was a tremendous flash of light, with a horrid smell like the sulfur from a spoiled egg. My, it stank like the dickens."

As Tom talked, we all leaned closer. Munch was so awed, his mouth looked like a big round donut.

"All of a sudden, I felt the floor flying up to meet me," Tom continued. "And lo and behold, I shrank right down to meet *it*, transformed, quick as lightning, into a small black kitten."

Then he explained how Dr. March Hall had snatched him up and zapped Tom and himself into the twenty-first century. From what we could gather, apparently, the doctor's plan was to turn Tom over to an animal shelter.

I don't think Tom really understood the business of the animal shelter but I figured that Dr. March Hall thought Tom would probably get put to sleep because there are so many unwanted kittens in the world. I guess this way, the creepy old guy could tell himself that he hadn't really murdered Tom, since he hadn't done the deed himself. Of course, there was also the possibility that someone would adopt Tom and never know he was anything but a cat. It's so horrible. And to think, we were having dinner with this creep just the other night.

Well, as we know, even as a kitten, Tom's brain was always on overdrive.

"Well, I was in a sure enough fix then," he went on. "But I spent my time in the doctor's hands, studying the possibilities. And by jings, I knew my chance would come."

His chance did come, as Dr. March Hall was opening the door at the animal shelter and had to temporarily loosen his two-handed grip on Tom. Immediately, Tom sunk his sharp little teeth into the doctor's finger. As March Hare reacted, Tom leaped out of the doctor's hands as far as his little legs could take him and zipped out into a parking lot.

There were so many cars parked in the lot, Dr. March Hall wasn't able to figure out under which one Tom was hiding. Not that Tom knew it was cars he was hiding under, never having seen cars before. It was all buggies and carriages back in his time. All he knew was that there were lots of convenient hiding places underneath these big metal contraptions.

As Tom talked, things started to fall into place because my dad's medical office is in a building just down the block from the animal shelter and it shares a parking lot with it.

"I was scared to death of all the queer noises," Tom told us. "But I had a bigger fear of being recaptured by old Mr. Smarty."

I stifled a guffaw at that one.

"So, I kept moving 'neath what I now know were cars, to try to put as much distance as possible between myself and that chicken-hearted March Hall. And then by Jiminy, the most peculiar thing happened. I saw an open door that had little clouds of pink and white smoke puffing out of it, and . . . well, hang it all, I can't explain it, but I got the notion that there was . . . aw . . . *goodness* on the other side of that door and help for the fix I was in."

And with that, his face got kind of red . . . and so did my dad's. They both sat back down at the table.

So Tom made his way to that open door . . . which happened to be my dad's office back door. It had been left open to let out all the puffs of smoke that were coming out of my dad's ears, because he had just discovered (he thought) a cure for Witch Flu. And my dad had seen this adorable trembling little black kitten and had brought Tom home that night as a surprise for me. And what a surprise he had turned out to be.

But listen to how creepy this is. All the time my dad was asking Dr. March Hall for help with Tom, poor Tom knew that the doctor was doing things to make things go wrong but he had no way of telling us. With the enchantment on him, he wasn't able to point out what a bad guy Dr. March Hall was, so instead he just took to hiding whenever the doctor came over. And that night, when Dr. March Hall pretended to have stamped on a spider . . . he had actually been trying to stomp the life out of Tom!! Just the thought of it made the cake and soda and ice cream in my belly start to churn and I felt really queasy.

So while we were away in Hawaii, Tom had been having a perfectly nice time, coming up with alchemical formulas on the computer, when black clouds started rolling in through the closed doors and windows again. This time though, Tom knew what was happening and he hightailed it out of Mom's office, raced upstairs, and found a place to hide that he hoped Dr. March Hall wouldn't think to look into.

He'd made a really smart choice (big surprise–I mean, he is a genius), because Dr. March Hall, who's too mean and nasty to have ever bothered to play with any children, thought the bulging hand puppet was just another stuffed toy. And that's what saved Tom as a raging, storming, violent Dr. March Hall tore our house apart looking for him.

This time, Dr. March Hall kept reciting the spell he planned to use on Tom when he found him, as if he was still trying to memorize it, and Tom happened to recognize it, from reading Dad's witchy medical textbooks. That horrible man was planning to turn Tom into a rock and he was going to toss him out into some field. Nobody would ever suspect that the rock was anything but an inanimate object and Tom's great mind would have been lost to the ages. Instead, at school, we would have gotten stuck with Miss Linegar assigning us to study about the many brilliant inventions of one great, big, phony blowhard, Dr. March Hall.

CHAPTER 24

March Hare Skedaddles

We were all absolutely exhausted but with a mad, evil witch on the loose, there was no question of getting any sleep. So, although Mom doesn't like to do this very often because it might stunt Munch's and my growth if we don't get enough real sleep, she cast another, stronger, refresher spell on everybody. It felt like jumping into a cool pool on a very hot day, a bit of a jolt at first and then that pleasant feeling of being completely wide-awake and full of energy.

Mom and Dad got right to work sending out an emergency summons to the witchy authorities, including the most famous witch there is, Mrs. Dorothy Drake, who is really, really old, and really, really powerful. Unlike Dr. March Hall though, she's also nice and full of fun. She usually makes chocolates come out of Munch's and my ears whenever she sees us, which I'm actually a little old for, though I can't say I mind the candy.

Aunt Sophie popped in too. She had been at some sort of movie premiere or something, because when she got there, she was wearing a shimmery gown that showed kind of a lot of skin. Tom's eyes nearly popped out of his head. As soon as she realized how serious the circumstances were though, she zapped into something more conservative. It was still pretty fancy, but that's just Aunt Sophie.

"Kids," said Mom to Munch and me, "we're going to need to you stay out of the way tonight, but I think there's a lot you can learn from what goes on here, so you can listen in if you like."

"Okay, lovie-doos," said Aunt Sophie. "I'm more of a light comedienne anyway, and I think I'd be miscast in this sort of drama, so why don't all three of us just snuggle up on the couch and we'll watch everything from there."

Then she zapped us into our robes and slippers so we could be comfortable and cozy while we watched.

As we snuggled up with the sweet-smelling Aunt Sophie on the couch, we looked in through the dining room arch at the big meeting that was going on. Everyone was at the table, with Tom at one end and

Mrs. Drake at the other. My mom and dad were sitting on one side and there were four really serious-looking witches sitting on the other side. One of them was Dean Wilkins, the head of Witch University, where Dr. March Hall taught from before Dad even went there. Dean Wilkins was tall and thin and wearing a dark business suit. He looked as if he hadn't ever been out in the sun much.

The other three men were younger and were dressed almost alike in jeans and leather jackets. They were identical triplets, Mr. Terence, Mr. Thaddeus, and Mr. Theodore Mather, who, due to the fact that they were on exactly the same magical wavelength, were able to triple the intensity of a spell when they cast it together. They were a trio of grim, muscular witchy policemen, called up whenever there was evidence of crimes against magic, and when they were on your case, watch out. Even a witch with the strongest skills possible, like Mrs. Drake, could be overpowered when the Mathers joined their magic together.

Tom was the center of attention for hours as he got questioned about every single detail of everything that had happened to him.

"What time of day was this?"

"In what direction was he looking as he cast the spell?"

"Can you recall if he clapped as he chanted?"

Tom seemed to have a pretty good memory for all the details they were asking about. Though when it came to exactly what March Hall had said as he enchanted Tom, Tom wasn't as helpful as everyone hoped because of course his hearing wasn't too great.

Expressions on the faces around the dining room table got very dark as the story got told and retold. Even sweet old Mrs. Drake looked angry as she heard the part about Dr. March Hall trying to stomp on Tom.

"In all my years . . ." she muttered and then stopped.

By the time Tom got to the part of the story about having to hide in the puppet, Mrs. Drake looked positively furious. Then she closed her eyes and a red heat started to glow out of her. Munch got scared and snuggled closer to Aunt Sophie as the six other adults at the table and Tom moved their chairs back from the intensity of the heat radiating out from Mrs. Drake.

Aunt Sophie cuddled Munch to her and explained that Mrs. Drake was about to launch an all-points summoning spell, something she's the only one alive skilled enough to do perfectly. With it, she'd be able to find and haul Dr. March Hall out of anyplace he'd found to hide.

It got hotter and hotter in the room and the walls all around us started to glow, but then Mrs. Drake gave a great sigh and opened her eyes. Immediately, everything turned cool and comfortable again.

"He's somehow removed his imprint from the continuum, I'm afraid," she said.

As she spoke, I was struck by how frail and quavery and old her voice sounded, especially after having just felt the heat from the immense power of her magic.

There was a collective groan around the table and Aunt Sophie explained to us that everybody's job had just gotten a lot harder, since it would now take a lot of magical detective work to discover exactly where and when Dr. March Hall had gone.

"Oh no, no," muttered Dean Wilkins, straightening the tie he'd loosened when things got so hot. "I blame myself, Dottie. He'd told me he was making advances in cloaking necromancy, but of course I was so used to that blasted self-aggrandizement of his, I didn't give it much heed. I figured he'd be retiring soon anyway, so there was no need to look into it much. I see now it was a terrible mistake to do that. He's clearly found a way to cloak himself from us."

Just in case you're wondering, self-aggrandizement is like tooting your own horn . . . It goes pretty good with being a blowhard, if you think about it. Blow . . . hard . . . Toot . . . horn. See what I mean?

Too bad it wasn't the right time to crack a joke just then.

Mrs. Drake patted Dean Wilkins's hand. "Oh my dear, how could any of us possibly have anticipated something like this? You mustn't feel responsible."

CHAPTER 25

A Posse

Mrs. Drake took charge and started organizing everyone, assigning time periods for them to search. She figured Dr. March Hall had probably given up on finding Tom, since as far as he knew, Tom was still just a little kitten who couldn't communicate with anyone.

"I don't doubt that the doctor wishes to waste no time in establishing himself as the most important inventor of the late nineteenth and early twentieth centuries. So perhaps we should start our search by dividing those particular periods between us," she said.

Though I was dying to get involved, I knew better than to offer to help, because there was no way Mom and Dad were going to let me search for someone who'd almost murdered someone.

Actually, if you think about it, this search party was sort of the witchy version of a posse like they used to have back in the Wild West to catch bad guys. I whispered that to Munch and he liked the idea so much that he zapped a cowboy hat right onto his head. He conjured up a rope and would have done some lassoing with it, but Aunt Sophie quickly made it disappear and zapped up some cowboy action figures for him to play with instead.

As the search began, people kept popping in and out of the room as if they were lights turning on and off. Tom, who'd never seen anything like it, came and sat with us on the couch and just marveled at everything.

"But Miss Sophie, how can they search if they're only gone a moment?" Tom asked.

Aunt Sophie explained that the searchers might have spent hours or even weeks in another time but could calibrate their return to the twenty-first century at almost the very moment they left it.

"It's hard to get it exactly right, sweetie, and it takes a lot of energy, so it's a technique that's only used if it's really important," she explained. "Which it certainly is in this case," she added, giving his hand a little pat.

"I'm not that great at calibration, for instance," I threw in. "Though I could probably get better with practice."

"I'll bet anything your mother would tell you the same thing," observed Tom with a grin.

As you can see, Tom managed to notice a lot of stuff even while he was still a kitten. I gave him a poke for that one and he snickered.

As people kept appearing and disappearing and stopping to discuss what they'd found, or actually *not* found, all of the adults got more serious than they had been. My dad stopped pulling little pranks like suddenly materializing while standing on his head. Apparently, on their visits back into the past, they were starting to notice some small changes in the development of technology.

I knew I was supposed to stay on the couch, but a girl has to go to the bathroom sometime, doesn't she? On my way upstairs, I managed to detour around the coffee table so I could get close enough to the dining room to overhear Mrs. Drake as she popped in and started whispering really urgently to Dean Wilkins.

"Charles, I'm beginning to spot massive disruptions in the time continuum, aren't you?" she said very quietly, but with an extremely worried look on her face.

The dean's back was to me, so I couldn't actually hear what he said, but it was pretty clear from the way

Mrs. Drake's forehead wrinkled up at his response that he was noticing the same thing.

"Then we really haven't got much time before the damage begins," she answered with a heavy sigh.

Okay, maybe I didn't have to go to the bathroom that badly, so I hurried back to the couch. Munch was set up with his toys behind the couch now, but Tom and Aunt Sophie had spotted my eavesdropping.

Probably Aunt Sophie didn't approve of eavesdropping, but she'd have to be made of stone not to be curious. I started whispering the second I got back to the couch so that she wouldn't have a chance to reprimand me.

"Mrs. Drake is beginning to worry that if we don't capture March Hall and return Tom to his time quickly, there'll soon be damage to the time continuum," I hissed.

Tom looked confused by that and so Aunt Sophie explained.

"Simply put, sweetie, the whole present world could be changed because the past is different," she said. And it was easy to see from her expression that she didn't think it was going to be changed for the better either.

Everybody in the dining room was starting to look absolutely exhausted. The Mather brothers, who weren't big talkers at the best of times, kept popping back in together. Then they'd just look tiredly at each other, as if it was too much trouble to say a word. They seemed to understand each other without actually having to talk though, because they'd just look into each other's eyes for a second, shake their heads, and then zap right back out.

Though it had to have felt like a long time for the posse, it was only an hour or so for Munch, Tom, Aunt Sophie, and me before Mrs. Drake called another meeting. Aunt Sophie conjured up coffee and sandwiches and all of the adults sat down very heavily in their seats at the table. By now, poor old Mrs. Drake's voice was so tired and weak-sounding that everybody had to lean in to hear her.

"My, my," she said as she smiled sweetly at everyone sitting around the table.

She had a lot of wrinkles in her face and they all seemed to crinkle upward when she smiled, as if her smile just needed to take over her whole face.

"When I look at all the decency and integrity gathered together in this room, it gives me such comfort and assurance that this evil cannot possibly triumph. Why, just the fact that Tom sensed the goodness emanating from Marley's office, and understood that help was at hand, is proof enough that we can't possibly fail," she said. "Now Matilda . . ." (That's my mom, did I ever tell you her full name is Matilda?) "If you would be so good as to apply one more of those invigorating little refresher spells of yours on everyone, I think we'd be better equipped to hash out this thing."

My mom, who really does have a special talent for that sort of spell, quickly zapped one up. Everyone gasped and looked startled for just a second, and then they all got a lot more rested-looking.

Each person did a rundown on the summoning and searching spells they had cast all through the decades and Dean Wilkins did a fast calculation. (And the calculating was all in his head. I guess that's why he runs a whole university.) From what he figured out mathematically and statistically and all that, it was decided that Dr. March Hare *had* to have been in one of the places and time periods they'd visited but had somehow managed to cloak his presence.

"Oh dear," sighed Mrs. Drake. "It appears that we're going to have to devise a whole new plan of attack."

It was agreed that everybody would go back to their homes and offices and whatnot and that there would have to be conference calls and visits with other experts in the field and computer searches and all that sort of stuff.

Once all the jobs were assigned, Dean Wilkins crankily got up from the table.

"I'll be on my way. And let's hope that *someone* can come up with a way to counteract this filthy cloaking spell," he said. Then he nodded good-bye to the others and popped out for the last time.

Mrs. Drake was worried that maybe Dr. March Hall had gone back into a period of time before Tom had done any of his important work, so he could get the big jump on inventing stuff.

In that quavery little voice of hers she said to my dad, "You know, Marley, I had hoped that at the very least, the doctor would have the ethics not to unbalance the progress of science by advancing technology too quickly."

Of course, I was thinking the kind of guy who would try to stomp on a tiny furry little genius wasn't going to have a lot of principles about scientific progress, but I knew this meeting was for adults only and I'd better not say anything. Anyway, I liked that Mrs. Drake was so good and honorable herself that she tended to think the best of people, even if they gave her plenty of reason not to. Miss Linegar could certainly learn a thing or two from her about giving people (such as, oh say . . . yours truly) the benefit of the doubt now and then.

So everybody said their good-byes for now and before they left, the Mathers put Tom between them and held hands to make a little circle around him. Then they chanted a complicated spell to put an extra-powerful protective conjuration on him to keep him safe in case old March Hare happened to come back looking for him.

My mom sadly told Tom that she was terribly sorry that he couldn't go home until Dr. March Hall got caught.

"Aw, don't get all vexed on my account, Mrs. Adams," he said. "The truth is, I'd hate to leave anyway, without having seen Abbie's play first."

Now it was my turn to get a red face. It made me feel pretty good, you know . . . that in the middle of all this creepy stuff that was going on, Tom was thinking about my play. The truth is, I hadn't given the play a thought for days, but now that I *was* thinking about it, I was really glad Tom was going to see it.

CHAPTER 26

Tom Discovers a Time-Warp

Well, with Mrs. Drake, Dean Wilkins, and the Mathers working the case, Mom and Dad figured they'd try to get us back to some sort of normal life for a while. That meant Munch and me going to school as usual on Monday, Mom organizing the PTA fund-raising dinner and studying her real estate stuff, and Dad getting back to trying to figure out what was the problem with his Witch Flu serum.

We'd been seeing quite a lot of the Schnitzler brothers lately, and Mr. Heatherhayes was making plenty of unscheduled visits as well. Dad was getting very worried about them, especially Mr. Heatherhayes, because of his age. While Mom made calls to people about bringing food for a PTA dinner, she flipped her way through her real estate books. Dad kept stepping into a time warp so that he could get a lot of work done without taking too much time away from his patients.

Let me tell you something I learned from having to go into the time warp myself on an occasion or two. (Mom tends to give us time-outs in the time warp as consequences for various things Munch or I might have done wrong.) Even though my dad doesn't seem to mind them, those time warp study sessions are no fun at all.

Listen to this:

Picture having detention in a room where there's nothing but a desk, a chair, and a ton of schoolbooks. Then picture yourself sitting there for days straight, studying. There's no time out for eating, or drinking, or resting, or even for going to the bathroom, because time stands still there and you don't have to do any of that.

When any of my time warp time-outs were over—trust me—I always felt that I had made up for whatever I had done wrong and *then* some.

At about noon on the Sunday after the posse left, my dad came out of the time warp to have lunch with us. Tom asked him a bunch of questions.

"You don't mean to tell me, Dr. Adams, that if I stepped into this time warp, I could get two weeks of study done while only a few seconds pass in the normal world!!???"

"Yup. That's about right, Tom." My dad smiled.

Well, Tom dropped the sardine sandwich he was eating, turned to my parents, and began to stammer.

"Oh, jingoes, might I . . . do you think it might be possible . . . would it be asking too much to . . . to . . . spend some study time in this time warp myself?"

So my parents put him in. And then, when he came out just as my mom was handing me my grilled cheese sandwich, he grabbed up a lot more books and asked if he could go in again . . .

Then, as I was taking my first bite, he came out, packed up all my parents' magic textbooks, and took *them* in with him.

Then he came out and asked if he could bring a computer in. After that, he showed up long enough to ask if he could set up a little chemistry lab, got Mom to zap him up all the stuff he needed, and went back in *again.*

The last time he popped out into the kitchen, he came tearing over to my dad, who was just finishing up his coffee and a last bite of brownie. Tom was so excited that he didn't notice Munch pushing out his chair to get up from the table and he tripped right over him and went flying.

"Oh! Bother! No, no I'm perfectly well thank you . . . I'm fine . . . Please don't vex yourself, Munch, 'twasn't anything at all," he sputtered as everyone rushed over to help pick him up.

"Dr. Adams, I've believe I've gotten results for your flu serum!!! Well, um, that is, at first I got about ten thousand results for things that *don't* work, but now I think I found one that will!"

All the rest of that day, Tom and my dad huddled together in my mom's office and then Dad zapped them both over to his medical office, where they huddled some more. After they zapped back home for dinner, they spent the whole evening huddled together in front of the computer until my mom finally put her foot down.

"Marley Adams, if you don't let that boy get some sleep I am going to turn that computer into a feather bed and I am going to toss him right into it!" she said very sternly.

Soon after, as Munch, Tom, and I stood together at the bathroom sink, brushing our teeth, I looked at the dark shadows under Tom's eyes and said, "Well, you certainly put in a hard day's work."

And you know what he said to me, with his tired eyes shining? He said, "Oh, Abbie. So far, I've never done a day's work in my life. It was all fun." And then he raced Munch down the stairs to say good night.

Next day, the huddling and calculating and figuring went on for even longer and all I could really understand about any of it was that apparently Dad's version of the Witch Flu serum was very, very close to what it should be but that it needed a little more something or other, a better balanced whatdoyoucallit and a dash less of whatever. Also, apparently, it needed to be refrigerated overnight.

When they'd run all their calculations about a million times, Dad went into the time warp with Tom so they could run them a few million times more. Finally, Dad, ears chugging pink and white smoke, announced he felt confident that the cure for Witch Flu was really figured out and it would be okay to administer to people.

It was decided that the Schnitzler boys and old Mr. Heatherhayes would be the first to receive the new, improved serum. Aunt Sophie popped in to share the great day. She zapped all Mom's vases full of congratulatory flowers.

The patients were supposed to come at four thirty,

but at four o'clock Munch heard a muffled yelling from inside his toy box and the Schnitzler boys popped out of it, pounding on each other, as usual. Apparently, back at home, one of them had taken more than his share of a piece of cake they were supposed to go halvsies on.

Mom separated them, gave them a little talking to about fighting, and then conjured up half a piece of cake each for them. Mrs. Schnitzler, their mom, zapped in shortly after, all out of breath and looking worried sick. She seemed relieved to see her kids and even more relieved to see that they weren't fighting for a change.

Mr. Heatherhayes's son arrived a minute or two later, wondering if we had seen his dad. So a search was begun and we found Mr. Heatherhayes sitting in Mom's pansy garden, looking confused. His son helped him up.

"It's all right, Pop. Everything's okay. I've got you now," he said tenderly.

As my mom followed everybody into the house, I saw her give a backward glance to her flattened pansies and flip a little healing spell on them with a wiggle of her foot. They straightened right up.

Inside the house, Dad introduced Tom to everybody and explained how Tom had finally figured out the right formula for the serum. The Schnitzler brothers couldn't have cared less about meeting Thomas Edison. But they were absolutely thrilled to meet Aunt Sophie, who had starred in their favorite movie as a pair of twin superheroes. They kept asking when her sister was going to arrive, and even when Aunt Sophie tried to explain about split screens and special effects and computer graphics, they really didn't seem to get it.

Mr. Heatherhayes and his son, on the other hand, were absolutely floored to learn that Thomas Edison himself had helped to formulate the new serum. A tearful Mr. Heatherhayes kept shaking Dad's hand.

"You really shouldn't have gone to all the trouble to get Edison himself in on this for us," he said over and over.

Dad made one or two attempts to explain, but Mr. Heatherhayes was so overcome with emotion that it seemed better to everyone to just let it go.

Dad administered the serum to the Schnitzlers first, through a needle to the arm. They howled at the top of their lungs for a second or two, then they stopped abruptly and got very still.

"I feel better," said Phil.

Then Felix shook his head a little. "I feel better too," he said.

Dad had them try a few simple spells, moving things around magically, turning objects into other things, and then finally zapping themselves in and out of rooms all over the house. Pretty soon it was obvious that all of their powers had returned. Dad asked them lots of questions and they both said they felt none of the faintness they used to feel when they lost their powers because of the flu, or the dizziness they'd feel just before they'd pop into places involuntarily after Dad's old serum had returned their powers.

Mom served cake to Mrs. Schnitzler and the Heatherhayeses while Dad and Tom stepped into the time warp with the brothers and came back a minute later saying they had passed every test and were definitely cured.

First the Schnitzlers hugged each other, then they hugged their mom, and then they turned themselves into puppies and chased Munch all the way up to his room to play. Their mom couldn't stop thanking everybody and crying and thanking everybody again, and crying some more. Mom and Aunt Sophie actually cried a little too, and I even felt my own eyes

filling up. That kind of thing is sort of catching sometimes, don't you find?

Next was Mr. Heatherhayes, who, because of his
age, was really in delicate health. Before he gave him
the shot, Dad washed a lot of healing and strength-
ening spells over him to make sure he'd be strong
enough for what was going to happen next. Mr.
Heatherhayes held his son's hand while Dad gave
him a shot in his other arm, and he winced a little as
the shot went in. Within seconds though, a healthy
pink flush came into his cheeks and he started to
laugh.

"I feel twenty years younger!" he yelled, and he actually got up and did a little jig.

Off they all went to the time warp to run the tests
and when they came back, there was no longer any
doubt. Witch Flu was cured for good.

CHAPTER 27

A Few Ribbits Too Many

Well, I could go on and on about all the celebrating that took place. That night, Mrs. Drake and Dean Wilkins held a special ceremony at Witch University, where they awarded Dad a lot of honors and zapped his and Tom's findings into all the witchy medical books. They couldn't give Tom a lot of credit though, because of course they didn't want the March Hare to learn that he wasn't still a little kitten. But Tom didn't seem to care.

All the witches who got cured from the new serum that had been zapped out all over the world started sending thanks. Hundreds of presents and cards and various other tributes kept materializing all over our house so that you couldn't take a step without tripping over something. Soon they had started to take up so much room, Mom had to miniaturize them all so they could be stored in a box in the basement and looked at later.

Even though Dad kept telling all our visitors that Tom really came up with the final formula, Tom always argued that he never would have been able to do it if Dad's original formula hadn't been so close to start with.

I watched Tom during these conversations (and there were a lot of them because we had dozens of happy and excited visitors). His slightly oversized head always had a huge smile on its face. It looked as if he was just glowing with happiness—but there was something sad behind it all too.

Meanwhile, the witchy posse was still hunting the March Hare so Tom could go home to his mom.

Back at school, I was happy to see Callie but it felt crummy too because there was so much I wanted to tell her about and I wasn't able to share any of it. It was kind of depressing, actually. What's worse, in all the excitement I had forgotten about a couple of pages of math work that I hadn't finished at school on Friday and was supposed to do on my own time.

You know what? My feeling is that even if she *did* know a terrible disease was being cured at my house over the weekend, Miss Linegar would *still* have as-

signed me four extra pages for homework as a consequence for not finishing the work. I mean, what
are saved magical powers compared to making sure
Abbie Adams never gets out from under her homework load????!!!!

It turned out Munch was having a few of his own
adjustment problems after such a wild few days.
From what he told me, I guess he wasn't able to sit
still in his seat in class for most of the morning. Mr.
Merkelson put him in another time-out, but I'm
happy to say that Munch was able to control himself.
Well, except for turning Mr. Merkelson into a frog
very, *very* briefly.

"It was really quick, Abbie. I swear," claimed Munch.

Well actually he said, "I thwear," but you know
Munch.

"I'm pretty sure he thought he just was having a
dizzy spell or something and nobody else even saw it!"
he vowed, his eyes all round and innocent.

The only reason Munch was even *telling* me about
it was because Mr. Merkelson still kept saying "ribbit"
at odd times throughout the day and Munch couldn't
figure out how to fix it. I'd have to imagine that by
the end of the day, that little "ribbit" thing was getting
kinda confusing to poor Mr. Merkelson.

So, after school, Munch asked me what he could have left out of his retransformation spell to leave the "ribbits" behind like that. I easily helped him fix it by firing an anti-vocalizing spell in through the window at Mr. Merkelson as he was tidying up his desk before going home. A couple of clicks and a whistle and no more "ribbits."

Munch was looking upset because he figured he was in trouble again, but he perked up when I said, "Don't worry, Munch, since you fixed it right away, I don't see any reason to tell Mom and Dad about what you did."

After all, I thought Munch had done pretty well at controlling his anger for once and we can't really expect him to be perfect.

Mr. Merkelson smiled at us as he came out the door and ruffled Munch's curls for a second. You know, he really is a nice guy. Hopefully, the next time he gives Munch a time-out, Munch will just go outside quietly and think about his behavior like he's supposed to—although I wouldn't bet a lot of money on it, would you?

We had a nice surprise when Tom turned up looking slightly stiff and awkward in a pair of jeans and a T-shirt my mom must have zapped up for him.

When he saw us, he ran over excitedly and started bouncing up and down on his new sneakers.

"Hello, Tom," I said.

"Hello yourself! Munch! Abbie! Would you look at these? What a bully idea to give shoes rubber soles! And to think of giving them treads, too! I've been sky-larking all over the streets in them. Have you any idea whose notion it was?" he bubbled as he bounced.

I noticed a couple of kids giving him a strange look, so I hushed him up the best I could.

"Hey, you wanna take a look around?" I asked.

I figured he hadn't seen too much the last time he was at the school, being stuck in my pocket most of the time. Munch grabbed his hand and hauled him off to the tetherball pole.

Now, Munch is pretty good at tetherball but Tom, not being a particularly athletic sort, didn't show a lot of talent for it. He kept getting bopped in the head and yelling "Confound it!" until he grabbed the ball, started experimenting with different angles of hitting it, and testing various speeds and heights.

Soon he'd figured out exactly how hard to hit it and where to put his hand on the ball. He was excitedly explaining it all to Munch using all kinds of ten-dollar words. To Munch I think it sounded like this . . .

"Blah blah blah, trajectory, blah, blah, blah, momentum, blah, blah . . ." It wasn't long before a bored-looking Munch grabbed Tom by the hand again and hauled him off to his favorite anthill instead.

A baseball practice was going on at the field, and on a water break Callie came over to see who Munch and I were hanging out with. Thinking quickly (and lying to my best friend yet again) I introduced them.

"Oh hey, Callie, I want you to meet my cousin Tom who's visiting. Tom, this is my very best friend, Callie."

As she smiled at Tom, Callie's expression changed.

"Tom," she said with a perplexed look in her dark brown eyes. "Have we ever met before?"

I actually thought it might have been funny if Tom had said, "Oh yes, but I was a kitten at the time," but of course he didn't.

He just said he didn't think they had met and started peppering her with a whole lot of questions about the rules of baseball. I guess it was a fairly new sport in his day. The whole time, he was talking so fast that Callie could hardly catch up with him and all at once, she just erupted in giggles and offered to come over and give him a few lessons while he was still visiting. I knew she'd like Tom. It's hard not to.

We left Callie to her practice and headed on home. As we opened up our front door, we spotted a man across the street, getting into his car. He had one of those little receivers stuck in his ear, and was talking to someone over his cell phone.

"Um, Abbie . . . I know I ask you this heaps of times," whispered Tom to me, sliding glances over at the man as we walked in the door. "But sometimes it isn't so easy to sort out. Magic or technology?"

"Technology," I answered, with a wink over to Munch. "But here's a little magic for you."

And with that, Munch and I each grabbed one of Tom's arms, flew him three feet into the air and up the stairs, with him screaming "Oh here, now!! Jingoes!! Oh jingoes!!" all the way up.

CHAPTER 28

Inspiration versus Perspiration

Upstairs, in my room with Tom, I threw my backpack on the bed and groaned. "Six pages of science, three math sheets, and one short story synopsis. Let me tell you something, Tom, I wish I was a genius like you, so all this stuff wouldn't seem like such hard work."

Tom's face was still flushed from the excitement of his flight up the stairs. "Rubbish," he grunted, excitedly pulling out my textbooks from my backpack. "Let me tell *you* something, my bully girl. Genius happens to be one percent inspiration and ninety-nine percent perspiration. You know, for two cents, I'd do all your homework for you, but then your mother would skin me alive. So what d'you say we just have ourselves a gay old time doing it together?"

He plopped himself down on my desk chair with

his arms behind his neck and his feet on my bed. "And now, please be a brick and define what a food chain is for me."

And you know what? It *was* kind of fun, because he got so excited about explaining things to me whenever I didn't understand. And when we were finished, he dug out my play script and ran lines with me, and raced all over the room, playing all the other parts. Which got kind of hilarious when he tried playing the mushroom and the caterpillar that was sitting on it—at the same time.

Next day at drama club, I had my part down so well I didn't make a single mistake in my lines. By now we were working with some of the lights and Miss Overton's "fantastical effects." There was this big screen called a scrim, which came down and pictures got projected onto it and you could see us walking around in front of it, looking as if we were in this weird, mystical place. There was also eerie music now and this really cool effect where a light turned off and on, really fast. It's called a strobe light and when we moved while it was working, it looked as if we were moving all choppy like robots or like we were in a strange dream. For the scene where the mushroom keeps coughing over the caterpillar's pipe smoke, the stage filled completely up with dry-ice smoke as if we were moving through a cloud.

You know what? This stuff really *was* fantastical like Miss Overton said and dare I even say it??? *Magical*– in its own way. When all the lights went down in the auditorium and then came up on the stage, where I was in my costume pajamas, reading in my big card-board bed, it was so exciting to me that it felt just like it does when the magic charge builds up in my fingers and starts buzzing all through me.

Back at home, I told Tom all about how great rehearsal had gone.

"That's grand, Abbie," he said, bouncing up from a book he was reading and giving me a high five like Munch had taught him. (By the way, the book looked about a thousand pages long and he was already three-quarters of the way through it.) "By Jiminy, I believe your performance is going to be a great achievement."

Of course, I started to think about some of the achievements I knew *he* had coming and how this big scientist once said that Thomas Edison basically *invented* the twentieth century, and I wasn't so sure about that. Still, it was clear that Tom really meant what he said.

"Well, gee," I said, going all red in the face. "I could use a snack, couldn't you?" Mom had mini pizzas in the freezer, and Tom loved pizza almost as much as sardines, so we went into the kitchen and I popped a couple in the microwave.

Half in a trance from watching the pizzas turn round and round as the cheese started to bubble, he murmured, "Um . . . I can't quite seem to recollect . . ."

"Technology," I answered.

I was still thinking about that hug he gave me and how much I was going to miss him and I said, "You know, Tom, if it weren't for a lot of the things you're going to invent, most of these things we use every day wouldn't even be around. Like if you hadn't invented a system to get electricity into people's houses, we sure wouldn't be microwaving pizzas right now. And if you hadn't thought up a way to record sound, we wouldn't be hearing that heavy metal Munch is blasting upstairs."

"Oh. Bother," said Tom as he winced at the loud thumping of the bass. "P'raps I ought to rethink that one . . . once I finally think of it."

So we had a chuckle, and it's funny how this happens sometimes, right out of the laugh, I started to feel all sad and mushy. I just really wanted Tom to know how much I'd miss him once they located March Hare and sent him home to his mom.

"Hey, Tom," I said, looking down at my feet. "Thanks for teaching me that there's no substitute for hard work and I promise I'm going to try to always remember it."

And I know what you're thinking, but I *will* try too. But when I thought about how Tom wouldn't be around to help me . . . I didn't feel hungry for pizza anymore.

Holding a microphone in his hand, Munch popped out of thin air onto my lap.

"Abbie, have you seen my T-shirt with the chains on it?"

I went up and found the shirt for Munch under his bed, which he'd transformed into a big amplifier for the heavy metal concert he was pretending to give. I zapped the dust bunnies off it, whispered a little quieting spell on the roaring crowd Munch had turned his stuffed animals into, and went back down to the kitchen, where the pizzas were ready. They just sat on our plates though without Tom or me taking a bite.

Tom was looking really sad now too. He sat at the table with his knees jiggling. "Well, blame it," he said.

"Don't I just wish I could remember you all after I go home."

Of course we both knew that there was no way that could happen, so I didn't say a thing.

"I do miss my mother though," he said quietly, and his knees stopped moving. He glanced over at the photo of his mom he had downloaded from the Internet, which Mom had framed for him and put on the wall. Then he shook his head a little and bounced back up to his feet. "What d'you say we tackle a spell technique lesson now?"

And so we did.

Back at school, there were only two rehearsals left before Friday, when the play would finally be performed, and we had sets to finish building and a hard dance routine that I was still having a lot of trouble getting down.

At lunch Callie took me out in the yard and drilled me on my dance steps, which she'd picked up in about a second from watching one of the rehearsals. It looked so great when she did it, with all her braids dancing around in the same rhythm as her feet. Some people just have a talent for that stuff, but I have these long, skinny legs that always seem to get tangled up with each other.

Finally, I got the routine down perfectly for the very first time and then I did it over and over, and over again, to make sure I had it.

"Hey Abbie," laughed Callie, throwing her arm around my sweaty shoulders. "I've never, ever seen you work so darn hard before. Good for you!"

Of course I couldn't tell her that Thomas Edison had been teaching me that there was no substitute for hard work—and for about the ten zillionth time, I wished I could share more of my life with my best friend . . . then I remembered that after Tom left, I'd have nobody to really talk with about certain stuff.

It made me feel lonely.

CHAPTER 29

Stage Fright

On Friday morning when I woke up, none of that was on my mind. There was a strange, prickly feeling in my stomach as if I was very hungry, but the thought of eating made me feel queasy . . . or squeasy, as Munch always puts it. All I could think about was the play, and how Aunt Sophie was coming to see it and whether I'd forget my lines or tangle up my legs in the dance routine. I guessed this was what Aunt Sophie meant when she talked about stage fright, which she warned me most actors get at some time or other. All I could do was hope it didn't get any worse as the day went on.

School seemed to take a hundred years, but *finally* the last bell rang and Callie gave me a big good luck hug and told me she'd see me later, before I rushed off to the auditorium for our last rehearsal. I ran so fast that I was the first one there and got a few minutes alone.

I loved looking at the set that we'd painted ourselves and at the cardboard bed I'd be lying in when the curtains opened . . . even though when I thought about that particular moment—the curtains opening—my heart started to beat hard and the magic charge buzzed into my fingers again. Other people started coming in, and I stepped behind a curtain and shook it off really quickly so that nobody would start yelling about bees.

Miss Overton got everyone quieted down and announced, "Perhaps it might be counterproductive to run the play in its entirety. So in the interest of maintaining its freshness, I believe that we should simply focus on a few of our 'problem areas.'"

Yes, yes, my dance was one of the "problem areas," but because I'd done it a million times, I got through the whole thing with only one tiny mistake. Then Miss Overton ordered in pizza for the whole cast. Pizza twice in one week. Too bad my stomach was in a knot and I couldn't enjoy it.

While we ate, we all sat around talking about how nervous we were. I'd never actually seen Calvin or Dennis nervous before.

"Hey, you guys are big athletes," I said. "You get up

in front of people on sports fields all the time, so what are you so nervous about?"

Without even stopping to consider it, they both said at exactly the same time, "It's not the same thing."

I figured it had something to do with knowing they're really good at sports so it doesn't bother them if people are watching because they're not worried about making mistakes. I sure wished I could know if I was good at acting or not because I was *really* worried about making mistakes.

The play was supposed to start at seven, so at six o'clock Miss Overton gave a very dramatic speech. "Now, my young thespians, are you ready to join the pantheon of those greats who trod the boards before you?"

Aunt Sophie told me later Miss Overton was telling us that we'd be joining the ranks of all the great actors who had walked on stage before us. Those would be pretty big ranks, too, because theater's been around for thousands of years. You can still go to the library and get some of those plays the Greeks used to do a couple of thousand years ago.

Later, as the auditorium doors opened and the people who were gathered outside started to come in, Miss Overton hissed, "Fifteen minutes!"

Suddenly, an ice-cold stab of fear shot right through me. From the other side of the curtain, I could hear snatches of people's conversations as they took their seats—stuff like ". . . had her for theater arts in 1982" or ". . . traffic was backed up for two miles."

Then my heart started to beat even harder because I could hear my own family walking in and Munch asking, "Where'th Abbie? Behind that curtain?"

I stepped right up to the halfway mark of the curtain and held it together with one hand while I opened up a tiny parting to peek through. There were Mom and Dad leading Munch to a seat, with Tom coming in right behind them. They got good seats too, right in the middle, about four rows back, close enough for me to hear them. Mom put her jacket on the seat beside her to save a seat for Aunt Sophie.

The auditorium was about three-quarters full by the time my aunt came dashing in. All conversation stopped and everybody in the whole place turned to stare at her. Aunt Sophie's pretty famous, you know, and people in my town don't often see very many famous people, I guess, so she was making a big impression. She stopped for a second as she was making her way into my family's row of seats and noticed everyone staring at her, even though they mostly ducked their heads down and pretended they weren't looking.

Aunt Sophie looked around, gave a sigh, did the little shimmy that goes along with a lightweight transformation spell, and turned herself into a very plain-looking lady who bore no resemblance to the very glamorous actress that she really is. Then she did a quick wave over the audience, skimming a forgetting spell over them, and took her seat. My mom gave her a big smile and patted her knee.

They were close enough for me to hear them.

"Thanks, Soph. For letting this be Abbie's night," she said.

Aunt Sophie hugged her and did a little finger wiggle again, and when Mom drew back out of the hug, she was wearing an entirely different, much dressier dress. Nobody was looking in their direction now though, so it went unnoticed.

"I just saw that on Rodeo Drive and I knew it was perfect for you, Matty." Aunt Sophie giggled.

Kind of a lot of my mom's chest was showing though, and the moment she looked down and saw that, she zapped her own dress back on and waved another little forgetting spell around for anyone who might have seen the switch. Aunt Sophie rolled her eyes and Munch, Dad, and a red-faced Tom all snickered a little.

It seemed like no time at all passed before Miss Overton ran around whispering, "Five minutes! Five minutes!"

All at once, my mouth dried up so completely that when I started to stretch my mouth for some of Miss Overton's warm-up exercises, my lips got stuck to my teeth. I stepped into the wings and swigged from my bottle of water, but the second I did, my stomach clenched up and made me feel sick again.

I tried to remember why I wanted to do drama club in the first place, but nothing came to mind. Right now I wanted to be anywhere else in the world but here in the wings of this stage, and I deeply regretted having told Aunt Sophie, a real-life professional actress, about my stupid fifth-grade play.

Over and over, I muttered the first line of the play so that I couldn't possibly forget it. "Why would someone write a book about a boy who can fly? Boys can't fly. Why would someone write a book about a boy who can fly? Boys can't fly."

And then . . . Miss Overton loomed up out of the darkened wings, saying, "Places, please."

Well, my place was dead center in the middle of

the stage, in my cardboard bed. Quickly, I got into it, flipped away the magic charge from my fingers, grabbed my prop book, and lay back against my prop pillow . . . shaking all over with stage fright.

The auditorium lights started to dim down to blackness and the audience quieted so that there was soon absolute silence. I turned my eyes down to look like I was reading and then I could hear the curtains sliding open.

BAM!!! The stage lights went up.

Have you ever felt as if your brain has just seized up on you? You'd like to be able to think and you know there's something you really need to be thinking *about* but nothing happens up there in the old noggin at all?

Nothing at all.

That's what was happening to me just then. I couldn't remember one thing that I was supposed to say. It was as if there had been a paralysis spell cast right on my brain. No words came into my head. One second went by, then two, then three, and the play didn't start because I was the one who was supposed to start it, with my first line.

What was that line?? Oh no! What was it?? What was it??!! Four seconds, then five . . . and then a little flurry of tiny, silvery sparkles fluttered up from some-where around the fourth row of the audience. They were so small that if anyone in the crowd had noticed them, they would have just thought they were dust specks sparkling in the lights. I knew what they were though, and that they were coming from my aunt Sophie to save me. I took a deep breath, my fear broke, the lines came back to me, and I started the play.

"Why?" I asked, snapping my prop book closed the way I was supposed to. "Why would someone write a book about a boy who can fly? Boys can't fly."

From that moment on, I started to have so much fun, I couldn't imagine what I had ever been afraid of. After I delivered my line and pretended to fall asleep, Caetano came swooping in through the fake window in his Peter Pan costume and I gave such a startled reaction that people laughed out loud. In fact, as I went on playing my part, people laughed in all the places they were supposed to laugh. Do you have any idea how great that feels? Then they got very quiet during my sad song. For the caterpillar scene, they laughed so hard that Calvin and Dennis and I had to wait for all the noise to die down before we could deliver our next lines.

There was one bad moment when Aunt Sophie's

cell phone went off and everyone's attention turned to it, but she zapped it away immediately and did another quick forgetting spell so it wasn't even noticeable to anyone but me and my family.

And okay, yes, I did trip very slightly during one *extremely* complicated step in my dance, but I was having so much fun that I actually turned it into another laugh for the audience.

Time never flew so fast as it did during that one hour that we were on the stage. You'd have sworn somebody had put an accelerator spell on it. When it was over, every single person who had performed was smiling as wide as the Cheshire cat himself.

When the play ended, Caetano, Calvin, Dennis, and I were the last to take our bows and then we all pounded each other on the back and told each other how good we were. Finally, all the bowing and back pounding was over, and Principal Oh gave Miss Overton a bouquet of flowers and Miss Overton made a big swooping curtsey and the house lights came up so the audience could see to leave.

You want to know something funny? The truth is, even though it was so ironic to be playing a girl who didn't believe in magic, I felt as if I actually did learn the same thing that my character learned during the play. For the first time, I realized that there are all kinds of magic in the world. And that's with or without witchcraft.

I went racing down from the stage to everyone who was waiting, and the first thing I did was throw myself into Aunt Sophie's arms and whisper, "Thank you."

She pulled me back so she could look right into my eyes and she said, "Abbie. There's nothing to thank me for. You started your lines before my spell had a chance to reach you. You know that, don't you?"

And I realized she was right. Not one of those little silvery sparkles had landed on me before my brain finally started to work and that first "Why?" came out of me.

Knowing *that* made me feel better than ever, and when Aunt Sophie hugged me to her and whispered, "You, my love, are a born actress," well, there really wasn't any way in this world for life to be any better.

Callie ran up and hugged me and Munch gave me a very affectionate punch in the arm and Mom and Dad threw their arms around me. "I don't know what we're going to do with *two* actresses in the family," sighed my dad with a big grin on his face.

Then Tom, who'd been standing to the side, looking sort of sad and wistful about all the family stuff, stepped over with his eyes all shiny and whispered, "You were bully, Abbie. Just bully. Crikey, I can see you playing Juliet next." (That would be Juliet of *Romeo and Juliet*, in case you're not a Shakespeare fan, and just so you know, that's a pretty big compliment that Tom gave me there.)

I hated for the night to ever end but of course it did. Later, I lay awake in my bed for hours, thinking about two things: how much I loved every second of doing that play . . . and wondering if they were ever going to locate Dr. March Hall so my poor, sad Tom could finally get home to his mom.

CHAPTER 30

The Posse Locates March Hall

The morning after the play, the witchy posse showed up again and told Mom and Dad that they'd finally located Dr. March Hall.

Using some special incantations that had been formulated by Dean Wilkins at Witchy U, Mrs. Drake found March Hare in 1848, which was twelve years before he had kidnapped Tom. Already, time had shifted and wavered so that Tom, who should have been a year old at that time, wasn't even born yet.

Mrs. Drake had zapped herself into the leafy boughs of a tree big enough to hide her, right in the small Ohio town where Tom was born. She told us she'd sensed the bad magic right away, like the powerful stench of a rotten egg.

While Mom and Dad summoned Aunt Sophie to come keep an eye on us, Mrs. Drake turned to Tom and gave him a sweet little pat on the arm. "I promise you we'll have you home soon, dear," she said. She even zapped up a few chocolates for him, but she made them appear in his hands instead of his ears.

I didn't mind really, but I might have been a *tiny* bit jealous that Mrs. Drake thought that Tom was too grown-up for her to make chocolates come out of his ears. You know what I mean? I guess I kinda wished she saw me as grown-up too.

Meanwhile, Dean Wilkins was teaching his new in- cantations to the Mather triplets. Even though these three tough guys weren't exactly the type to get excited, they actually cracked a smile for once, and Thaddeus told Dean Wilkins he might just have revolutionized witchy law enforcement.

Once everyone was ready, the posse quickly zapped out. This time they didn't zap back in again till much later in the day, and they came back at slightly different times, because they were all too nervous to calibrate properly. Now everybody had something to eat and Mom and Dad filled us in on what had happened.

When they arrived at the time and place in 1848, which Mrs. Drake had found, they had disguised themselves as fence posts and trees and stuff like that. Everybody immediately got an unmistakable whiff of the bad magic Mrs. Drake had sensed. Even sensitive witches like my mom can't always detect individual acts of bad magic, but when there's a massive misuse of magic like was going on in that town in Ohio, any witch can detect it.

Mrs. Drake transformed the whole group into a flock of crows and they followed the scent to a laboratory, set up right on the outskirts of town. Dean Wilkins, who's like a walking fact factory, recognized it immediately as an identical copy of Edison's lab in Menlo Park, New Jersey, picket fence and all. The way things were actually supposed to happen, that lab didn't get built until 1876 and it's where Edison invented so many things that he got over 400 patents in the seven years he worked there. Oh, nothing too important, mind you, just little items like the long-burning lightbulb, the systems to deliver electricity, the phonograph, a mimeograph copy machine, and even a megaphone. Though when I think about how Miss Rogan storms around the schoolyard with her megaphone, yelling "Walk!! Walk!!" to anybody who's running around having fun, I kind of think we could have done without that one.

Hey. Doesn't the fact that he built the Menlo Park lab just go to show you how unimaginative Dr. March

Hall really was, despite all the big brainpower he was always bragging about? He couldn't even think up a lab of his own to build, he had to steal that from Tom too. I wondered if when Dr. March Hall "invented" the phonograph, as he was doubtless intending to do, he'd record himself reciting "Mary Had a Little Lamb" the way Tom had.

The search party sniffed out all sorts of spells that Dr. March Hall had already cast in the area, all strictly prohibited by witchy law, unless for self-preservation or the protection of another witch. For instance, he'd implanted false memories into the minds of the people in the area so that everyone would think he had lived there for years and that they'd seen him building the lab over time, rather than it just popping into sight, as it actually had.

That sort of thought manipulation spell requires really entering the minds of people, something that's a terrible, terrible invasion of privacy. How'd you like some creepy guy like Dr. March Hall poking around in your private thoughts? When witches do things like zap little forgetting spells on people, that's a necessary and elementary sort of spell that even Munch can do (at least some of the time) and it doesn't mess with people's minds much. To actually get in there among another person's thoughts to create false memories is the worst sort of misuse of magic and if you ask me, it's just incredibly rude besides.

With the posse members gathered around my family's dining room table again, they started to figure out how exactly they were going to capture March Hall. By the time most of the talking and planning had been done, it was long past Munch's and my bedtimes again, and this time Mom wouldn't even discuss putting on a refresher spell. Munch had fallen asleep on the couch, so he didn't complain when Dad carried him to bed, but I couldn't believe that I wasn't going to get to see what happened next.

Still, off to bed I had to go, but Tom, being two measly years older and the subject of all this stuff, got to stay up. Actually, he hardly seemed tired anyway. Some people just don't seem to need as much sleep as others, I guess, though sometimes while Tom was staying with us I had seen him catch little five-minute naps over the course of the day. Hey, I guess you could call them "cat naps." Maybe it's something he learned when he was enchanted.

I lay in bed with my brain buzzing and wishing, wishing, wishing that I could be a part of it all.

And now let me just say this. I swear that I absolutely meant to stay in bed and go to sleep like my mother wanted. It's just that I thought that it would be only fair (and I'm sure you'd agree) that I should get to hear at least *something* about what the actual strategy was for capturing Dr. March Hall. I mean, it was my kitten he almost stomped, wasn't it?

So I snuck out of bed. And really, I just meant for it to be for a moment. But from my bedroom doorway and then, darn it, even from the top of the stairs, all I could hear was a quiet murmur of voices, going on for almost an hour. Then there was a little buzz of activity, and by poking my head over the stair rail, I could see that the whole search party had all popped out at once.

I could see Tom go into Mom's office, where his bed was, and Aunt Sophie started coming up the stairs. Yikes! I didn't have time to run into my room, so I zapped myself into bed and lay there trying not to breathe too hard because I'd had to do it so quickly.

First I could hear Aunt Sophie going into Munch's room to make sure he was covered, and then she came into mine. I lay there, as if dead asleep, and she pulled up the covers and gave me a light kiss on the forehead.

She always smells so good, my aunt Sophie. It's

from some sort of perfume she gets whenever she zaps over to France. Anyway, after she kissed me, she went back downstairs and started cleaning things up and turning down lights. By hooking my feet on the stair railings and lying down flat on the stairs, I could get myself close enough to actually hear what she said when she poked her head into Mom's office.

"Tom, lovie. They'll be needing you at Menlo Park for a bit, so I think you'd better get what rest you can right now. You try to close your eyes and I'll be just as quiet as a mouse out here."

What? I thought. They're coming back for Tom? Tom is going to get to go to Menlo Park and I'm not???

I didn't *mean* to have these jealous thoughts. But I ask you, how can a person control their thoughts?

Once, I saw this movie where these kids wanted to sneak out at night, so they stuffed pillows under their blankets to make it look like they were still sleeping in their beds. Actually, come to think of it, I've probably seen it about ten different times.

Well, I hated to use a cliché, so I gave it a little twist of my own, by zapping up a life-sized doll that looked just like me, and tucking it nicely into my bed. Just to be sure that it looked real, I swept the doll's long brown hair over its face, so that from the doorway or wherever, there'd be no reason to think that it wasn't really me under there. Of course, if Aunt Sophie decided to plant another kiss on my forehead there'd be a problem, but I figured one good-night kiss a night is probably the usual thing.

Then, *ZAP!!* I zapped myself into a whole heap of trouble.

CHAPTER 31

I Hitch a Ride I Shouldn't Take

Tom didn't even look startled when I materialized at the foot of his pullout bed in my mom's office. He wasn't asleep, of course. He was reading as usual, still with his shoes and sweater on.

"Yep. I'da bet anything you'd never stay in bed," he said with a smug little grin.

"Okay, you got me. I'm a little nosy," I countered. "Now what the heck's the big plan?"

"Crikey, Abbie. It's all so int'resting. I've just been reading up on it. Look here."

He showed me the page he was studying in a University Level Witch Textbook.

I took a look.

Yikes. There were words like "malfeasance" and phrases like "bi-level, simultaneous decontamination of inter-dimensional, corruptive machinations."

I tried to get my head around what I was reading, but it might as well have been written in Chinese.

"Okay, genius. Can you explain to me what any of that means?"

He took the book back from me.

"Well, I guess what it pretty near means is that I'm going to have to be there when they catch old Mr. Smarty, so that they can do spells on us both at the same time to clean up all the bad magic.

"But, Abbie," Tom went on gravely. "You know you're my true blue friend and a fella never had a better one. Still, I can't let you come with me, because I am so beholden to your mother and father and I know they don't want you anywhere near that rotten, wicked man. Crikey. They don't want *me* anywhere near him either, but it can't be helped."

I understood. Of course Tom was never going to disobey my parents, or put me into any sort of dangerous position . . .

And that's why I wished him luck, said good night to him, zapped out . . . and materialized as a tiny version of myself, right inside his sweater pocket.

Tom had hardly had time to settle himself back with his book when my mom zapped into his room.

"Are you ready, sweetheart?" she asked.

I sank back farther into the warm wool of Tom's pocket, hoping she was in too much of a rush to sense anything out of place, magically speaking. My hopes came true, because Tom barely had enough time to answer before there was a great whoosh of air, and he found himself in Milan, Ohio, circa 1848. He was standing behind a hedge, a few hundred yards away from the buildings of Thomas Edison's famous Menlo Park lab.

Only in this case, it was Dr. Smarty March Hall's *not* so famous Menlo Park lab.

Peeking through the loose weave of the sweater pocket, I recognized the lab from Tom's and my Google searches. I could also see various bushes, trees, and picket fence posts around it that could possibly be the posse members—or that might just be bushes, trees, and picket fences. Still, Tom and I were so far away from the lab that there was no chance of me seeing what was going on.

"Hide here for now, dear," said my mother to Tom worriedly. "The Mathers have warned us that Dr. March Hall may have set up booby traps and we don't know what to expect just yet. I'll be back for you the moment we feel it's safe to get you."

My mom zapped away and Tom ducked down into

the bushes . . . where I couldn't see a darned thing from inside his stuffy pocket.

I couldn't stand it, I just had to see what was going on. So, shaking with nervousness, and maybe also from a very guilty conscience, I zapped myself out of Tom's pocket and back to my normal size, behind the lab building, where I found a window near a corner. Back in the distance, I could see Tom, still hunkered down, unaware that he'd ever had a stowaway in his sweater.

Through the window, I spotted old March Hare, working with glass tubes and wires and things. He had lots of helpers and everybody was busily bustling around and seemed pretty excited about what they were doing. Well, why wouldn't they be? Hello? They were about to help with one of the most important inventions of all time—the long-burning lightbulb.

I didn't have to have a university level witchy education like the one Tom gave himself, to figure out that the most logical way for the ambush of Dr. March Hall to start was for the Mather triplets to get together to throw a gigantic time freeze on the entire lab.

Sure enough, there was a strange waver in the light. Ants, crawling on the window ledge, froze in place. A beaker, which had just been knocked off a table, hung in space, and the workers in the lab suddenly stood stock-still.

Because they can move in and out of time freely, witches aren't susceptible to time freeze spells. So a moment or two after the time freeze took hold, I saw old March Hare glance up from his work and suddenly notice nobody else was moving. It was sort of funny actually, because he jumped about a foot into the air with shock. I almost giggled because it looked like the kind of jump I once saw Mom do when Munch popped a balloon right behind her back.

Unlike Mom though, old March Hare didn't start laughing. Uh-uh. He began storming around in a huge rage, knocking over his own lab tables and roaring out stuff like "NOOOOO!!!" and "HOW??? HOW COULD THIS HAPPEN??!"

It was scary, let me tell you. I'd never seen an adult lose control of their behavior like that, and I made really sure that I couldn't be spotted by the doctor as he raged around the lab.

Pretty soon there was a shimmer in the corner of the room and some delicate violet particles like flower petals started floating about. It was Mrs. Drake, quietly making her presence known so that she wouldn't startle March Hare too badly. And he did quiet down as he focused on the spot where she was starting to materialize.

Now that there wasn't a lot of yelling going on though, I couldn't catch much of what was being said because the windows were closed. It looked to me as if Mrs. Drake was calmly and reasonably talking to Dr. March Hall. I imagine she was trying to convince him to give himself up.

That's just like her, you know, hoping that people will do the right thing if given the chance. But it was clear from the ugly stare that old March Hare was directing at her that he wasn't likely to do that. Then Mrs. Drake made a big mistake. She stepped toward him.

All at once, some kind of horrible force came slamming into her, as if an invisible wall had come crashing down. She cried out and crumpled right down to the floor. I gasped.

I'd just seen my first witchy booby trap in action.

Now, as I stood paralyzed in shock, I saw my dad zap into the room at hyper speed, whisk Mrs. Drake up in his arms, as if she was as light as Munch, and zap right out of there with her. My heart was pounding through my chest and I stood frozen as inside the lab things started to happen really fast.

Appearing in tight formation, Mom, Dean Wilkins, and the Mather triplets flashed into sight and surrounded Dr. March Hall on all sides from about ten feet away. They threw their arms out, as if they were reaching for each other's hands, and started chanting. Even muffled like it was through the window, it sounded really, really scary. I'd never seen a dark look like that on my mother's face in my whole life, and let me tell you something, I hope I never see it again.

Dr. March Hall screamed without words and slammed his arms out and every time he did it, Mom and the other witches lurched back as if they'd just walked into an invisible electric fence.

Whoosh!! Booby trap number two exploded in everyone's faces. Flames surrounded March Hare. This time everybody was ready, and their energy shields forced the flames down until they disappeared.

Oily, black smoke started billowing up underneath Dr. March Hall's feet, so dark and thick that he began to disappear. All the while, Mom and the other witches chanted their weird and scary spell, slowly pushing their way forward through what seemed to be March Hall's magical force field. I couldn't make out much of what they were saying but I can tell you this: The word "CRUSH" kept coming up. Yikes!

March Hare's force field seemed to be getting smaller under the strength of the other witches' powerful, combined magic. I knew that once they got close enough to actually grab each other's hands, the Mathers could triple their power, and we wouldn't ever have to worry about March Hare again.

Well, I've been wrong plenty of times in my life. But I've never been as wrong as that.

CHAPTER 32

Dad Gets into Terrible Trouble

All my attention was glued to the window, so it took me a second to notice the foul smell of sulfur that strangely wafted past my nose. I knew exactly what it meant. I leaped behind a bush around the corner of the lab so fast that I couldn't have done it any faster if I'd zapped myself there.

Less than five feet away from me, black smoke bled out into the air, from out of nowhere. Flickering in and out of physical form inside of it was the enraged and raving Dr. March Hall himself. By great good luck, he was facing the other way from me and he was writhing and shaking as if he was straining to do something that required enormous strength. Then, before I'd had a chance to think about what move I should make, *POP!!!* he emerged fully formed out of the smoky air and took a hard fall to the ground.

The doctor picked himself up and looked around in shock. An evil mutter came from his tight mouth: "Not here. Not here. Not here!!"

He started trying to zap himself somewhere else but he just kept sputtering in and out of view. I guessed (and hoped) that all the magic directed at him when he was inside the lab had weakened his powers. Who knew for how long though?

Trying not to make a move that might be noticed, I shot a quick glance inside the window. From there, I saw that the black smoke was still filling the gradually shrinking space inside of the circle Mom and the other witches were forming. They were still pushing as hard as they could against the force field and reaching for each other's hands. It was clear that they thought Dr. March Hall was still inside of that thick cloud of smoke.

I was quickly running over my options in my head, when something just terrible happened.

My dad, back from taking Mrs. Drake home, materialized, *right in front of Dr. March Hall!*

It was all so fast that Dad didn't even have a chance to realize what had happened before Dr. March Hall grabbed him with both hands and slammed his forehead right into my dad's!!

Then, in this horrible growl that hardly even sounded like talking, he cast a paralysis spell on him and there my dad stood, bleeding from the head but completely frozen. Right away, all that fury that March Hare had been spitting out all over the place got focused, absolutely terrifyingly, right on my completely helpless dad.

"You! YOU!" he raged as he stormed back and forth in front of my dad. "My own student! My protégé! You'd turn on me? You'd betray me? What is it to you, if I take a little something for myself? Not ethical enough for you, good Saint Marley? Does the student think that he can teach his teacher? Oh, how ironic. Well, here's a little more irony for you, you ungrateful snake! After having wasted my brain power on teaching you, I'm going to wipe your mind absolutely clean now. You'll be nothing but an empty shell for the rest of your tiny, suburban life. They can use you to hang hats on!"

BOOM!!! A vial of some horrible, gray-looking potion zapped right into March Hare's hands.

I'd never loved my dad so much in my life as I loved him just then. As I saw what terrible danger he was in, all the spit suddenly dried up in my mouth. A huge magic charge shot into my fingers and buzzed so powerfully that my hands started to jerk around like they were on marionette strings. I couldn't think about that though, because I had to figure out how to help my dad.

There was no chance that anybody inside the lab could hear me through the window, over that deafening hum, even if I screamed. On the other hand, if I zapped in and tried to explain what was going on, it would take so long that March Hare would have time to wipe Dad's mind.

The only thing in my favor was that old March Hare loved to hear himself talk and he was still taunting Dad, and complimenting himself on the "delectable irony" of it all. All the time he was doing this, I was thinking as hard as I ever have in my life. But it was no good. I couldn't remember the exact sequence of the paralysis spell that's geared for an adult witch.

"Stomp the feet? Click the tongue?" Thoughts streamed through my mind, but nothing seemed right. My brain started to seize up like it did when I had stage fright. And time was running out for my dad!

And then I got help.

"Two clicks of the tongue, Abbie girl. One stomp of the right foot, visualize four cubes of ice, and thrust both hands before you."

It was Tom.

I'd never, *ever* been so glad to see anyone.

With Tom's arm around my shoulders, I felt as if I had nothing to worry about. My mind switched into hyper speed as the whole formula snapped into my brain. As soon as it did, I leaped out, with Tom, from behind the bush and screamed at March Hare, "Leave my dad alone!"

Then I whipped my hands out in front of me and fired off the spell.

∞

Well, I guess it's safe to say that both March Hare and I received very big surprises simultaneously. March Hare, because Tom and I had just jumped out at him. And me . . . because that nervous, magic buildup in my hands, which I should have remembered to discharge before trying to fire a spell, blasted out of the ends of my fingers, jerking my hands way up in the air.

My spell missed Dr. March Hall completely.

Well. It felt as if time had frozen without anybody casting a spell. March Hare stood there, agape. (That means with his mouth hanging open, if you'd like the picture.) I just stood there too, completely paralyzed with fear.

But you know what? I don't think there was anything that could have made Tom stop thinking. In a heartbeat, he yelled "AAAAAHHHH!" at the top of his lungs, jumped right at March Hare, grabbed that vial of potion right out of his bony old fist, and tossed it to me.

"Get your mother, Abbie," he shouted. "Quick as lightning!"

With a horrible roar of rage and some words that I know my mother would rather I had never even heard, March Hare leaped right at me.

ZAP!

As fast as Tom told me to, I zapped myself into the lab behind me. And there, I screamed as loud as I could that Dr. March Hall wasn't *in* the cloud of smoke—he was out behind the lab and that Dad and Tom were in trouble.

There was a huge *WHHHOOOOSH* as all five witches instantly zapped themselves outside. Through the window, I saw that March Hare had his hands around Tom's throat, choking him, but the Mather brothers snatched Tom away and then tackled March Hare and wrapped themselves around him, giving him such a dose of combined magic that he passed out on the spot. They said a few words over him to make sure that he couldn't move when he woke up, and then they stood guard over him, looking pretty darn scary.

My mom was at my dad's side, stroking his cheek and whispering an anti-paralysis spell to him. As he came out of his frozen state, tears burst out of her eyes and she threw her arms around him and hugged him really hard.

Dean Wilkins made sure the wheezing, gasping Tom was okay, and then my mother rushed to Tom and fussed over him too. Then she and Dean Wilkins zapped back into the lab and appeared in front of me.

I was afraid to look at my mom.

As I handed Dean Wilkins the vial of horrible potion and explained what it was, I shook all over.

He immediately snapped a magical lockbox around the vial. "You're a very brave girl, young Miss Adams," he said.

That was nice to hear, but I knew this was one very brave girl who was in a whole lot of trouble with her mom right now.

CHAPTER 33

The Spaceship Incident

Well, I won't bore you with all the details of what happened once I had to discuss things with my mom and dad. I'll just say that it's a funny experience having someone so mad at you and yet so happy that you did what you did, they keep getting all mixed up between yelling at you and hugging you as hard as they can.

It's even funnier feeling so guilty for something you did and yet so happy that you did it, because you helped to save your dad.

While we were all there, and I was telling my side of the story, Mrs. Drake appeared in a flurry of violet petals, completely recovered from her bad experience with the booby trap. It all had to get explained to her, and somewhere in the middle of that, old March Hare finally opened his eyes. That's all he was able to do though, because he had one mega-potent paralysis spell on him.

Mrs. Drake, who's so fair that it's almost unbelievable, insisted on giving March Hare back his power of speech so he could tell his side of the story. When it turned out to be just exactly what everyone thought, that he had kidnapped and enchanted Tom, tried to kill him, and broken every other witchy rule in the book and wasn't even sorry for it . . . even Mrs. Drake had to admit that he was a pretty bad guy.

There and then, Dr. March Hall's punishment was decided by unanimous vote. Well, I didn't get to vote, but you can bet I'd have voted the same way if I had been allowed.

Mrs. Drake put Tom and the immobile March Hare inside a magical cleansing circle for the purification rite and there was a lot of chanting and spell casting that went on for quite a while.

Then, in what one might have called a "delectable irony" (if one happened to be an evil, mad, witchy scientist), Dr. March Hall got his memory erased by my dad, whom he'd been planning to leave completely mindless. Then his magical powers were stripped by the Mathers, who alone in all the witchy community have the power to perform that spell.

After that, Mrs. Drake personally zapped March Hare to a retirement community in a remote area of New Zealand, where he'd get three meals a day and bingo on Fridays. The March Hare was gone for good.

The Mather brothers stayed to oversee the return of the area to what it was before Dr. March Hall arrived, and to make sure that all the spells he cast got recalled and everything.

The rest of us all headed back home. We had to go slowly though, rather than zap right in, because Dad was pretty shaky from the head injury Dr. March Hall had given him and Mom was insisting that he have it X-rayed before he zapped the wound closed.

Dean Wilkins zapped ahead for a moment to let Aunt Sophie know that we wouldn't be back until later. Then he returned, to make sure we were doing okay with Dad. Myself, I was thinking that once Aunt Sophie heard that I was with the time travel party, she'd be checking my bedroom—and probably not liking what she found there.

The truth is, I really like time traveling slowly like that instead of zapping, which we usually do for convenience's sake. Even though it takes more time, you can see things changing in the world right underneath you. You see more and more houses being built, skyscrapers going up, planes starting to fly, seasons changing over and over—all that sort of thing. Even more fun, once you finally arrive at your destination, you seem to approach it from a great, great distance and you can watch what's happening there as you get closer.

This time, as we got close to home, we could see what was going on inside the house, but it all looked tiny, as if we were looking at it from far away. As we drew closer in time, we could hear everything being said, and the people and things began to seem to grow bigger, almost as if we were walking up to a movie screen. Well, it's funny that I use that simile. (And why is it a simile and not a metaphor, class? Why, because we used the word "as" or "like," Miss Linegar.)

It's funny that I used the movie screen simile, because Munch and Aunt Sophie, who had been waiting there so anxiously, had been trying to kill time by watching one of Aunt Sophie's movies. I knew this movie too—it was a big special-effects extravaganza.

The effects apparently impressed Munch, because he started trying to create the same sort of thing right there in the living room. And so all at once, an alien spaceship crashed up through the living room floor, causing Munch and Aunt Sophie to topple right down into the basement.

Leaving Mom and me to continue to support the still woozy Dad, Dean Wilkins and Mrs. Drake shot ahead, zapped away the spaceship, fixed the house, and made sure everyone in the basement was all right. They were, because a quick-thinking Aunt Sophie had managed to zap a big feather mattress onto the basement floor just in time to soften their landing.

When we arrived on the scene a few minutes later, Dean Wilkins and Mrs. Drake were out in the neighborhood, casting a forgetting spell on anyone who might have noticed the spaceship incident. Munch quickly turned himself into a potted plant to try to avoid Mom's wrath, but she told him he could just take his time-out as a plant right now and that they'd talk later.

Well, at least I wasn't the only person in the family who was in trouble with Mom.

Aunt Sophie was too worried about Dad to pay much attention to me for a while, but once Mom had zapped in the X-ray machine from his office and Dad was being cared for, she turned to me with a wondering look in her eyes.

Right away, I said, "Aunt Sophie, I am really, really sorry that I snuck out on you and I'm really, really sorry that I ... well ... pretty much lied to you by putting that fake me in the bed."

"Yes, that *was* pretty much lying, my love," Aunt Sophie responded sadly.

Facing up to what I did was one of the hardest things I ever had to do, and you know why? Because I could tell it really hurt Aunt Sophie's feelings that I would lie to her.

Oh man. I hurt my aunt Sophie's feelings, which is the last thing I'd ever want to do. I really *was* sorry, I can tell you, and I made a pact with myself to try to prove to her that I would never do anything like that again.

Well, Dad turned out to have a slightly fractured skull but Dean Wilkins had no problems healing it, and everyone had to tell and retell the story for Aunt Sophie . . . with Munch listening from his flowerpot. When it got to the really scary part about the attack on Dad and Tom getting throttled and the mind-erasing potion and everything, Munch morphed back to himself very quietly and crawled into Dad's lap.

Mrs. Drake sat down and took Tom by the hand very sweetly. "Let me explain, Tom dear, what will happen next. You will be returned to exactly the moment in which you left your own time. Your dear family will never know that you've been missing. And it's regrettable for you, I know, Tom, but I have no doubt that you understand that due to the simple physics of time, none of your memories of your stay here will return with you."

"None at all?" asked Tom, really sadly, even though he knew the answer. His eyes moved over the books on the shelves, and over everybody in the room too, before landing most sadly right on me.

I thought about all those nights we'd hung out together with books piled up on the bed, a few sardines on a plate for him and cookies for me, and my eyes filled up with tears.

"Well, I suggest that we might as well get a good night's sleep before we start setting history straight." Mrs. Drake patted Tom's hand again and stood up.

Munch giggled when a couple of chocolates fell out of his ears. I reached up to see if there were any in mine, but she was looking right at me as I discovered there was nothing there.

"It seems you're quite an extraordinary young

woman, Miss Abbie Adams," she said, and she shook my hand just like I was all grown-up.

And you know what? I wouldn't exchange that handshake for a hundred chocolates . . . and anyway, Munch gave me some of his later.

Just in case you think that the whole episode was over and I had gotten away without any consequences for following the posse back in time, think again.

I've never had such a severe consequence in my whole life. First of all, I had to deal with Aunt Sophie's feelings being really hurt, which just about killed me. Even worse, Mom was determined to show me what a terrible thing I had done by disobeying her and Dad and putting myself in danger.

I got the lecture of all lectures, believe me, and because my bungled spell had almost gotten me and Tom killed, I had to go into the time warp where I did nothing but study spell technique for TWO SOLID WEEKS.

I'll say it again. TWO SOLID WEEKS!!

On the upside though, I caught up on a lot of witchy lessons that I had been letting slide of late. For instance, did you know that a buildup of magic charge in a witch's hands during stressful situations is a defense mechanism much like the one in which adrenaline floods through non-witches' systems when they face danger? Or, here we are again, the way a cat's tail puffs out when he's trying to make himself appear bigger to an enemy.

Well, maybe you might have figured that one out, but I'll bet you didn't know the twelve simple techniques for ". . . dissipating, directing, or diverting the defensive charge while casting a spell."

I know all twelve. And why do I know? Because I read all four chapters on the subject in the Level Five Spell Textbook. Six times.

Tom would be proud.

EPILOGUE

I woke up to the sound of a lot of people downstairs and with a jolt realized that today was Tom's last day. Feeling nervous and weird, I rushed to brush my teeth and get dressed. Before I started down the staircase though, I ran into Tom on his way up to see me and we sat together on the top stair.

Neither of us said anything for a while and then I bumped my shoulder against him.

"You know, I'm feeling pretty funny here, Tom," I said. "On the one hand, I really want you to go so you can start with that recording sound thing . . . because you know how much I *adore* it when Munch blasts heavy metal and everything. But on the other hand, I don't want you to go at all."

He smiled sadly and looked down at the floor, his knees jiggling. "Yes, hang it. It's all mixed up, isn't it? Here I am wanting to go home to my family, but feeling like I'm *leaving* my family at the same time."

He drew a little closer to me.

"Say, Abbie. I was studying on how you won't really have anyone to talk to after I go and that it might be powerful lonely 'cause you're obliged to keep secrets from Callie. So I had a notion there might be something about it in some older witchy books, ones that nobody much reads these days. Last night, I spent a week in the time warp and by jings, I found something that old Mrs. Drake herself wrote."

He opened up a thick, yellowed old book.

"Look here, Abbie, where I marked it. It says there are precedents in years gone by, for witches telling the secret."

He stopped for a second and grinned as he watched me trying to figure out what the heck "precedent" meant.

"Or let me tackle it this way," he said. "Ah . . . see . . . it's happened before, that witches haven't kept mum about magic.

"There's an old-fashioned precautionary spell that can be cast . . . You can figure *that* out, can't you, Abbie, 'pre' meaning before and 'caution' meaning carefulness?"

"Yeah, yeah, smarty-pants," I said, giving him another little shove with my shoulder. I happened to have learned all about that precautionary spell stuff during my TWO WEEK consequence. "Precautionary spell for what?"

"So they can't let on about magic! Even by accident! It's a bully spell, Abbie, bully! And I allow your parents will let you use it on Callie, if they talk to Mrs. Drake about it first!"

Then he pressed the old book in question into my hands, jumped up, and cupped a hand to an ear.

"But hark!" he boomed dramatically. "What on earth is that I hear? Why, it's the cry of the wild goodbyetoabbiegift! A noble and ferocious beast!"

Then he pulled open the door of the hall closet, reached down, and picked up something tiny and trembling that was mewing sweetly.

I gasped and reached out my hands for the adorable little gray kitten he held.

"Well, blame it all. I figured you got cheated of a pet when I got disenchanted, and your parents agreed, so . . . well, I hope you like her, that's all."

I sat there cuddling my new kitten and looking up at Tom while I tried to think of how I could show him how I felt about the gifts he'd just given me. But in the end, all I could do was say, "Thanks."

That was the last private moment I shared with

Tom, but it was a good one. There really wasn't much else to say but good-bye, and all the people gathered downstairs, from Mrs. Drake right down to the Schnitzler brothers, had come to say just that.

There was a lot of handshaking, quite a bit of hugging, and a few tears shed. (The tears were from my mom and Aunt Sophie . . . and, well, okay, from me too.)

Tom shook my dad's hand.

"Upon my word, Dr. Adams, it's rotten hard that I won't be able to remember everything you've taught me. It's been a bully honor, sir. Bully," he said.

Suddenly, there was so much pink smoke puffing out of my Dad's ears that Mom had to apply one of her smoke-clearing spells again.

Then Tom turned to Mom and his voice started quivering. "And M . . . M . . . Mrs. Adams. You were just as good to me as my own mother, and . . . and . . ." He didn't have to finish because my mom just gathered him up in a big hug that said everything he was trying to say.

Finally, he turned to Munch and picked him up, and Munch grew four more arms to give him the biggest hug of all. Then there were more hugs all around and more handshaking and stuff.

At last, Mrs. Drake, who was to do the honors, stepped up and said, "Now, Tom dear, I think it's time we got you back to your mother."

She put one of her thin, wrinkly hands on each of his cheeks, whispered a quiet little incantation, and just like that . . . he was gone.

Mom had a surprise for us though. Just as quickly as Tom disappeared from the room, Munch and I found ourselves disguised as fence posts, joined to a fence where I could sense Mom and Dad were also present. We were right next to a window in a makeshift lab, at the back of an old-fashioned house. Inside, Tom had just popped into view.

He looked dizzy, just for a second, and then he went happily back to the chemistry experiment he had laid out on his table, just as if he'd never been gone at all.

Later that morning, I sat in my room missing Tom and thinking about how I'd never turn on another light without remembering him.

Just then, there was a terrific *BOOM!* and a lot of smoke from across the hall.

Apparently, Munch had decided to start a little chemistry lab of his own. ∞